FATHER
TURIDDU
AND THE POLAR VORTEX

A NOVEL
— Third In A Series —

Daniel Conway

FATHER
TURIDDU

AND THE POLAR VORTEX

A NOVEL
— Third In A Series —

Riverwood Press
Louisville, KY

Daniel Conway is the author of three Father Turiddu novels: *Father Turiddu the Savior of the City*, *Father Turiddu Returns: the Cardinal and the Inquisitor* and *Father Turiddu and the Polar Vortex*.

Available at www.danielconwayauthor.com

Published by: Riverwood Press Louisville, KY
www.danielconwayauthor.com

ISBN-13: 978-1519423191

Cover and interior design by Jane Lee
Sketches by Mark Castillo, Photo on back cover by Mark Scott Abeln, Copy editing by William R. Bruns

Printed and bound in the United States of America

DEDICATION

This book is dedicated to
Monsignor Salvatore E. Polizzi and all
living and deceased members of the
Vito and Rosalia Polizzi family.

AUTHOR'S NOTE

This is a work of fiction. While it's true that many of the characters are based on real people, all of the situations depicted here are the work of my imagination. Names have been changed—ever so slightly—to underscore the fact that the characters are speaking and acting in a work of fiction.

Similarly, many of the places referenced in this work are based on actual sites, but I make no claim to accuracy in the precise location of streets or in the relative distances between one place or another.

In case any readers are confused about Father T's actual age, this is understandable because: 1) he looks and acts younger than he is; 2) he tends to advance his age by saying, "I'm nearly 83 years old," when he is, in fact, 82; and 3) the events described in this book—especially the so-called polar vortex—took place in January 2013 nearly three years before the manuscript was completed.

Finally, some readers may wonder about the significance of Father T's devotion to the Sacred Heart of Jesus (*Sacro Cuore di Gesu*). The *Catechism of the Catholic Church* (#478), quoting Pope Pius XII's 1956 encyclical *Haurietas Aquas* states, "Jesus has loved us all with a human heart. For this reason, the Sacred heart of Jesus, pierced by our sins and for our salvation, is quite rightly considered the chief sign and symbol...of that love with which the divine Redeemer continually loves the eternal Father and all human beings without exception." Father T, who was ordained in 1955, has maintain an active and very personal devotion to the Sacred Heart of Jesus for more than half a century.

DAY ONE
MONDAY EVENING

It was the worst winter storm Father T could remember. For most of his nearly 83 years of life, the city he loved had mild winters. Not this year. On January 5, Mother Nature dropped a foot of snow on the city. The next day the "polar vortex," a massive blast of arctic air, caused temperatures in Canada and the Midwestern and eastern United States to fall dangerously below zero, resulting in record low temperatures in North American cities as far south as central Florida.

"This is insanity," Father T said to himself as he looked out the window of his second-floor sitting room to the church parking lot below. His car, which was always parked in the space marked "pastor," was covered with mounds of snow. Underneath was a thick coat of ice.

"Thank God, I don't have to go anywhere tonight!" the priest exclaimed. "There's no way I would make it."

Monsignor Salvatore E. Turiddu, whom everyone called Father T, was assigned to his current parish in the city's central west end in 1981, 33 years ago. Most of his seminary classmates had long since retired, or passed away, but Father T remained an active, full-time pastor.

"As long as I have good health," he said frequently, "I'm going to use all the gifts God gave me to serve my people." Not only did he serve the people of St. Roch Parish, but Father T managed the affairs of his elderly and infirm sister Anne, and he helped out any number of individuals and families who depended on his help and guidance. He was also "on call" for a whole host of archdiocesan and civic responsibilities carried out on behalf of his archbishop, the mayor, the chief of police and even the local field office of the Federal Bureau of Investigation.

Only two years before, Father T had helped uncover and diffuse a domestic terrorist plot to blow up abortion clinics throughout the city. "I don't condone what goes on in those clinics," the priest said, "but the dignity of human life is absolute, and the end doesn't justify the means!"

A year later, Father T returned to his beloved Italy to help save his friend and former archbishop —now a prominent cardinal working in the Vatican—from left-wing "thugs" who had kidnapped him and held him hostage, demanding that he "confess" to the Church's crimes throughout history. Joining forces with Interpol and the Vatican's Security Agency, Father T (with help from family members and friends) freed the Cardinal from captivity and brought the international terrorists to justice.

It was no wonder that he was called *"il salvatore della città,* (the savior of the city)." He had earned the title years earlier when as a young priest he helped save the city's Italian neighborhood from the devastating effects of "white flight," the outmigration of whole neighborhoods due to fear and racial prejudice. "If you stay in your homes and don't give in to the fear mongers," the young Sicilian-American priest proclaimed from the pulpit and at neighborhood meetings, "no one can take them from you. End of story!"

Father T faced similar challenges when the old archbishop first assigned him to St. Roch in 1981. The parish was located in the city's central west end in a once prominent neighborhood that was almost completely abandoned by more than 5,000 people who sold their stately homes for pennies on the dollar and moved out to the suburbs. "The archbishop told me to save St. Roch," Father T always said. "He didn't tell me to save souls or rebuild the neighborhood, but how could I save the parish without serving the needs of the people—all of them—who live within the parish boundaries!"

Now, 33 years later, St. Roch was a thriving parish and school, and the neighborhood was once again a highly desired place to live and raise a family. Serious problems remained. (The crime rate was still high.) But Father T was justly proud of what he had accomplished in the past three decades—not all by himself, of course, but with the courage, hard work and generosity of many people, including a core group of parishioners and their pastor's large and influential network of family members and devoted friends.

Don Turiddu (as the priest sometimes called himself in deference to his Sicilian roots) was not so active at the moment. Sitting quietly in front of the gas fireplace installed for him during his first week at St. Roch by former parishioners from the Italian parish, the elderly priest murmured his evening prayers. His favorite prayer book, a carryover from his seminary days with faded ink, worn pages and large numbers of memorial prayer cards for deceased classmates, family members and friends, was on his lap. When his formal prayers were concluded, Father T spoke directly to the Sacred Heart of Jesus whose image looked down on him from the mantel over the fireplace.

"I'm getting old, dear Jesus, and I'm very tired. I can't handle this harsh winter. Why did you send this to us now after all these years? Thirty-three years ago, maybe, but not now, Lord!"

The Sacred Heart didn't have a chance to respond before the rectory phone rang, startling Father T so much that his old prayer book slid from his lap and hit the floor scattering prayer cards all over the sitting room floor.

"Good evening, St. Roch," Father T said.

"Oh, Father, thank God you're home. This is Mary Castelucci. Mother has taken a turn for the worse. She's dying."

Mary Castelucci was a nurse at Saint Mary's Hospital. Her mother, Andrea, was one of Father T's oldest parishioners, a founding member of the Ladies of St. Roch, and the parish's first "bereavement minister" in the days when helping families cope with death was not just an official Church ministry but everyone's Christian duty.

"Have you called 911?" Father T asked.

"Oh, no. Mother won't hear of it. She wants to die in her own bed, not in a hospital. But she desperately wants to see you, Father, and receive the last rites. Can you please come"?

"I'm not sure I can get there, Mary," Father T said sadly. From his earliest days as a priest he had never said no to a parishioner in need of pastoral care. "It's what we do," he always said, "and it's who we're called to be—priests who bring Christ to others especially in their greatest hours of need."

"I know, Father, it's a terrible night. I wouldn't dream of asking you to come if it weren't so important to mother. Please do what you can."

"You know I will, Mary. It may take me a while, but one way or another I'll be there. Tell Andrea to hang on as long as she can."

"Thank you, Father. God bless you!"

The priest hung up the phone and stared across the

room at the image of the Sacred Heart on the mantel.

"Is this how you answer me? I get the message. No more talk about being old and tired. I need to get out of this chair and go do what I was ordained to do almost 58 years ago—minister to the sick and dying no matter how inconvenient it is for me personally."

"Just tell me one thing," Father T prayed. "How in the heck am I supposed to get to Andrea's house? I can brush off the snow from my car, and maybe crack enough ice to open the driver's side door, but I'll never make it out of the parking lot—let alone through streets covered with a foot of snow. It will take the city a week to get around to these side streets, and at these temperatures everything underneath the snow will be a sheet of ice."

The Sacred Heart didn't respond to Father T's questions. He simply allowed the priest time to consider his options and choose for himself.

"I can't call Vinnie or Mike or John," he thought to himself. His priest friends weren't close enough and would never get to him in time. "Sam, our maintenance man, has an old car that would never make it in this weather. Is there anyone else I can call—someone who lives close by who owns a SUV with 4-wheel drive?"

Father T picked up the phone and called the president of the parish council on his cell phone. "John, I know you're on vacation this week and are missing all this horrible weather, but I need help. Can you think of a parishioner with a 4-wheel drive vehicle who could help me get to Andrea Castelluci's house? Mary just called. Andrea is dying and she wants me to come right away and anoint her. My car is covered with snow and ice and the streets are impassible."

John Ford had been president of the St. Roch parish

council since before anyone could remember. "I'm the pastor, and I appoint the council president," Father T would say when anyone asked him about term limits. "John is doing a splendid job. I see absolutely no reason to replace him. Let the next pastor pick someone new. End of story!"

John thought about telling Father T to stay home. (He had been watching news reports of the awful "polar vortex" back home.) But he knew Father T too well to think he would ever say no to a parishioner in danger of death. He remembered the time many years ago when an overly zealous nurse (at a Catholic hospital!) had tried to prevent the priest from anointing one of his parishioners right before surgery.

"You can't go in there," the nurse said, pointing to the double doors the led to the operating room."

"Excuse me?" Father T replied. "That man is my parishioner. I'm going to anoint him and say some prayers. It won't take more than a minute."

"I'm afraid that's not possible. Visiting hours are over."

"Visiting hours? I'm not a visitor. I'm his pastor. I'm going to go in there, anoint him and pray with him before you operate."

"I'll have to check with the surgeon," the nurse said. "Wait here."

As she went into the room, she pushed a button and the double doors opened. They remained open as she conferred with the doctor and came back out again.

"I'm sorry. You can't go in there now," the nurse said pressing the button to close the doors behind her. But the doors remained wide open no matter how hard, or how many times, she pressed the button.

"I'm only going to say this one more time," Father T

said. "That man is my parishioner, and I'm going to anoint him and pray with him before he has surgery. End of story."

"I'm calling security," the nurse said. The doors remained wide open and Father T could see his parishioner lying on the table being prepped for surgery. The nurse stood in the center of the doorway with her arms folded—as if to suggest that she would physically prevent the priest from entering the room. But no matter how often she pressed the button, the doors simply would not close.

Two security officers arrived.

"Sir, you must leave the hospital," one of them said menacingly.

"I'm not going anywhere. That man is my parishioner. I intend to anoint him before he has surgery."

"Then we'll have to carry you out," the other guard said.

"Let me warn you," Father T said with his eyes flaming and his words cold as ice. "I'm Sicilian. If you so much as lay a finger on me, or touch me in any way, my brothers and cousins and nephews will hunt you down. Believe me, they'll know how to handle you."

The two guards looked at each other, but they didn't touch him. Instead, they called the hospital's chaplain, a priest who knew Father T well. When the chaplain arrived and asked what was going on, Father T said one more time, "That man is my parishioner, and I'm going to give him the last rites before he has surgery."

With that, Father T walked through the still-open doors and anointed his parishioner. End of story.

John Ford suggested that Father T call a young parishioner, Sean McEnroy, who was an active member of the parish council and the men's club.

"Good idea, John. I'll give him a call right away. Thank you. Give my best to Kathy and enjoy your vacation in Belize. Please pray for me—especially as I head out into this awful winter storm."

Father T looked up Sean McEnroy's number in the parish directory. Before he placed the call, he prayed once more to the Sacred Heart. "Jesus, please don't let me put this young man in harm's way. He has a wife and young children. My time is limited, but please, Lord, keep Sean safe for a very long time!"

"Sean, this is Father. Are Christina and the children safe from this awful storm?"

"Yes, Father. The children are in bed and Christina is studying for a test tomorrow. The university probably won't be open, but she wants to be prepared just in case by some miracle classes are not cancelled."

"You're sure everyone is safe?"

"Very sure, Father. Why do you ask? Is something wrong?"

"I need your help, Sean, but I'm embarrassed to ask for it. Andrea Castelucci is dying, and she's asked for the last rites. My car is completely covered with snow and ice, and there's no way I can get there by myself. John Ford would take me, but he and Kathy are in Belize. He suggested you might be able to help. But I don't want to do anything that would cause problems for Christina or your children."

"Father, you know I'll help you. How soon do you want me to pick you up?"

"As soon as you can, Sean. I don't know how much time Andrea has left."

"OK. Normally it just takes me a couple of minutes, but tonight you better give me 20. I'll meet you in front of the rectory's front door. I don't want to mess with the parking lot. The streets are bad enough."

"God bless you, Sean. I'll be waiting at the front door."

Father T gathered the holy oils and the ritual book for the Church's last rites. Then he bundled himself up with several layers of clothing, grabbed his winter hat, scarf and gloves, found the snow boots he had worn on his last ski trip (at least 20 years before) and walked out the kitchen door and down the steps to the back entrance of the church. The snow was so deep, and the ice underneath it so thick, that it took him a long time to travel just a few feet. When he got to the back door, he took the glove off his right hand and reached into his pocket for his keys. It was bitter cold, and as he pulled them out his hand trembled and he dropped the keys in the snow. The backyard light had been out for several months and, as a result, it was pitch black. Looking down at the snow, all Father T could see was darkness.

"Jesus, Mary and Joseph!" he exclaimed. "How stupid can I be! Why didn't I have Sam fix this blasted light months ago? St. Anthony, please help me find these keys."

Digging around in the snow was frigid and frustrating work, but St. Anthony interceded and Father T found his keys after a few very cold minutes. He unlocked the back door, climbed the narrow steps to the sacristy, and then went into the sanctuary of the church to remove the sacred species from the tabernacle. The priest opened the tabernacle door, genuflected, and took four reserved consecrated hosts from the ciborium and placed them in a small receptacle called a pix. (One host was for Andrea, one for Mary, one for Sean and one for himself). Then he reversed his steps and returned to the rectory—making sure to keep a firm grip on his keys as he locked the back door of the church and opened the rectory's kitchen door.

"Sean should be here by now," Father T said to himself. "Getting the sacrament took a lot longer than I thought it would!"

The priest went to the front hallway and attempted to look out the front door's window. He couldn't see anything. The glass was frosted and when he attempted to wipe it off all he could make out was swirling snow.

"Look at how that snow is blowing! The wind chill has to be in 10 degrees or more below zero! This is insanity!"

He had no choice but to open the front door and look out. There were illegally parked cars in front of the rectory packed with the same snow and ice that covered Father T's car in the church parking lot. But as Father T looked to his left to the space immediately in front of the church, he saw a large SUV with its lights on and its windshield wipers struggling to keep the snow off the windshield.

"God bless Sean. What a good man he is!"

The snow on the rectory's front walkway was so deep that Father T found himself trudging through an accumulation that was knee deep. As soon as Sean thought he saw the priest coming (it was hard to be sure because of the blowing snow), he got out of his vehicle and tried to help him. It was slow going for both of them. Finally, they met half way—on what should have been the sidewalk but was now a mountain of fresh snow—and Sean helped Father T work his way through the snow to the passenger side door of his SUV.

"Do you know where Andrea lives?" Father T asked his young friend once they were both inside the vehicle that was desperately blasting hot air through its vents in an effort to fight off the bitter cold outside.

"Washington Terrace, isn't it?"

"That's right. I think we should take the parkway. There's a much better chance the city will be plowing there. It's a major artery."

Sean put his SUV in gear and slowly edged away from the curb. Visibility was poor—impossible really—so the young man drove the SUV at a crawl carefully down the street praying that no one else was foolish enough to be driving or, God forbid, walking in the neighborhood on this Godforsaken night.

"Turn right here," Father T said. "This will take us to the parkway."

Sean did as he was told, but it was a blind act of faith. There was no way he could tell for sure whether he was turning onto the correct street or entering some alley.

"It's only a block to the parkway. There's a traffic light there. We'll need to turn left."

The snow continued falling as the Chevy Suburban crawled forward. Father T had never driven a vehicle this large. He was a reluctant driver to begin with. (He didn't get a driver's license or own a car until after he was ordained a priest.) He hated the city's rush hour traffic and carefully timed his trips to avoid dealing with the madness. Whenever possible, he let his younger cousin, Msgr. Cugino, the pastor of the Italian parish, drive. Now he thanked the Sacred Heart that his young parishioner was doing the honors.

"Watch out, Sean. The light is right in front of us!"

Sean applied the brakes too quickly and the large vehicle went into a spinning slide. Fortunately, there were no other cars near them and they came to an abrupt stop up against the curb and pointed in the wrong direction.

"I'm so sorry, Father. I'll be more careful from now on."

"Don't apologize, young man. No one in his right mind should be driving under these conditions. It's not your fault."

Slowly, the SUV made a U-turn. It reminded Father T of a battleship or cruise ship making a long, slow about-face in deep water. The light was green, so Sean kept moving across the intersection to what he hoped was the eastbound lane of the parkway.

"This is going to be a long trip," the young man thought to himself but didn't say out loud. "I hope we make it."

Their left turn onto Union Avenue was only four intersections down the parkway, but at the rate they were going they knew it would take a while. Sean's attention was on the road ahead, or what little he could make of it. Father T tried to count the intersections as they passed through them. It was impossible to read the street signs or recognize the area. They were literally "flying blind."

Just as they approached Union Avenue, they saw flickers of light in the near distance ahead. Sean slowed to just a few miles per hour. As they got closer, the lights appeared to be flares warning them of trouble ahead.

"What's the problem?" Sean asked.

"I can't tell," the priest answered. "But it looks like trouble."

A car in front of them had stopped and turned its flashers on. The blinking lights of the car combined with the burning light of the flares to create an eerie visual accent to the white falling snow. Sean stopped the SUV and strained to see what was ahead. No use. They could barely see the car in front of them. Everything else was a total blur.

"I'm going to have to get out and see what the problem is," Sean said. "Please stay in the vehicle, Father. There's no sense in both of us freezing to death."

"Nothing will happen to you, young man. The Sacred Heart promised me that I would bring you home to your family safe and sound. But be careful all the same!"

As Sean opened the door a blast of bone-chilling cold air assaulted him. At that moment he was especially grateful that his wife, Christina, had bought him a heavy, hooded coat for Christmas. At the time, he thought it was an unnecessary extravagance. In his 29 years of life, he had never worried much about winter. A few cold days each year was the norm. But nothing like this arctic cold— and all this snow!

After Sean left, Father T sat quietly and prayed. There was no point straining to see out the windows. Flashing taillights, the glow from flares up head and blowing snow were all he could see. A couple of minutes passed, and Sean did not return. It was too soon to worry, but Father T began to feel very much alone.

A faint vibrating in his shirt pocket alerted the priest to an incoming call, but by the time he undid his coat and removed several layers of clothing in order to retrieve his cell phone, the call had gone to voicemail. His caller ID told him the message was from Msgr. Cugino. The voicemail he left said, "Sal, this is Vince. Call me."

Father T pressed the "call back" feature, and a few seconds later his cousin answered.

"Where are you? I called the rectory and you didn't answer. Don't tell me you've gone out in this storm!"

"I had to, Vincenzo. Andrea Castelluci is dying, and she's asked for the last rites. How could I possibly say no to her? You know what she's done for St. Roch— and for me."

"I understand, Sal, but why didn't you call me? You can't make it to her house on your own."

"I'm not alone, Vinnie. Sean McEnroy was kind

enough to pick me up in his SUV. Right now we're sitting on the parkway near Union Avenue. There's some kind of problem up ahead, and Sean went to see what it is."

"For Christ's sake, Sal, be careful. And call me if anything happens."

"I will, Vinnie. I promise."

It was another 20 minutes before Sean returned. (Father T was watching the clock on the dashboard of the Suburban.) When Sean opened the door, he was covered with snow and shaking badly.

"What happened?" Father T asked. "Are you OK?"

The young man struggled to speak. His face was bright red. His eyebrows, ears and nose were icicles.

"I think I'm OK, Father. There was an accident. A bakery truck was stuck in a snowdrift and it was blocking the intersection. Two of us—the driver of the car in front of us and I—had to push from behind while the truck driver rocked his vehicle back and forth until it finally cleared the intersection. I don't think that truck will get very far tonight, but at least it's out of our way."

"You're a good man, Sean. I'm sorry I got you into this."

"We do what we have to do, Father. You taught me that a long time ago when I was a student at St. Roch School."

The car in front began to move forward and its lights stopped flashing. For the first time since they had stopped, Father T noticed that the flares were gone, replaced by an even thicker blanket of white.

Sean inched the SUV closer to the intersection using low gear.

"Turn left now!" Father T shouted, causing his young parishioner to flinch before carefully easing his Chevy Suburban onto what he hoped was the right side of Union

Avenue.

As far as they could tell, there was no traffic in either direction as they crept north on their way to Washington Terrace.

"There's the bakery truck on the right," Sean said as they passed what looked like a massive mound of snow parked on the side of the road. "I hope the driver makes it home OK."

"The entrance to Washington Terrace is up ahead on the left," Father T said, "but it's not going to be easy to find in this whiteout."

Sean kept his SUV crawling forward. He tried rolling down the window on his side of the vehicle to see if he could get a better view of what they were passing on the left, but the open window didn't afford much of a view. In fact, the swirling snow (driven by the powerful arctic air) formed a thick screen that made clear visibility hopeless.

"Up ahead," Father T said. "I think I see the archway that marks the entrance to Washington Terrace. Slow down."

"I can hardly go any slower," Sean thought to himself, but he took his foot off the gas pedal and allowed the Suburban to coast.

"I'm right. It's the archway. Turn left—now!"

The large SUV glided to the left, its rear wheels sliding on the sheet of ice packed beneath the foot of snow on the roadway. Sean compensated nicely, and they passed under the archway into one of the city's most prestigious older neighborhoods.

"Gianni Castelucci made a ton of money in the wholesale fruits and vegetables business," Father T said to his young companion. "He was always generous to the Church and to anyone in need. Andrea has continued that tradition for the past 25 years since Gianni passed away."

Father T counted the houses on the right, which were barely visible, until they reached number 7. "This is it," he said. "Don't try going in the driveway. Just stop here."

Sean got as close as he could to the curb, which was discernible only by the mounds of snow created by plowing earlier in the day. That forced Father T to exit from the driver's side. The passenger door was blocked by the snow and would not open wide enough for even a thin and wiry man like Father T to squeeze through.

Once again, Father T thanked the Sacred Heart for his young parishioner. Only by supporting one another (with Sean doing 90 percent of the supporting) were they able to trudge through the 12 inches of accumulated and blowing snow to get to the front door.

Father T rang the bell, and within seconds they were greeted by Mary Castelucci.

"Thank God you made it safely, Father. Mother has been waiting for you."

"Good evening, Mary. Do you remember Sean McEnroy? I never would have made it here without his help. He is truly an angel of mercy!"

"Of course, Sean. Welcome. Thank you for helping Father T get here safely. Please let me take your coat—and yours, too, Father.

Andrea Castelucci was lying in a hospital bed in the front parlor of her stately old home, which her nurse daughter had transformed into an infirmary. She was sleeping quietly when her daughter escorted her pastor and his young friend into the room.

"Andrea, it's Father T. Don't try to speak. Just pray along with me silently if you can."

His friend and parishioner opened her eyes and smiled. Father T invited her to kiss the crucifix that her daughter had placed by her bedside—next to her rosary. He then used the holy oils to anoint Andrea's body making the sign of the cross on her forehead and her hands.

Father T said the prayers and administered the holy Eucharist to Andrea, Mary, Sean and himself with all the dignity and respect due to a child of God whose life had been a blessing to all who knew her.

"May almighty God have mercy on you, forgive you your sins, and lead you to everlasting life," the priest prayed while reading from the ritual book.

"Go home to God peacefully," the priest prayed to himself. "You've lived a long and faith-filled life. You deserve to be with Jesus and with Gianni and your parents."

Andrea smiled again as though she had heard his silent prayer. Then she whispered, "God bless you, Father," closed her eyes and went back to sleep.

"It won't be long now," Mary said. "I can't thank you enough, Father, for coming out on such a horrible night. Can I make you a cup of coffee or give you something to eat? I hate to send you both back out there with empty stomachs."

After looking at his companion to see if he wanted something, Father T declined Mary's generous offer. "You stay with your mother. We'll be on our way. But please call me if you need anything."

"God bless you, Father. And, Sean, please drive carefully. I wouldn't be able to live with myself if anything happened to you or Father T tonight."

The trip back to St. Roch was slow going but uneventful. When they arrived in front of the rectory, Sean helped his pastor walk to the front door.

"I owe you big time, my friend. Be sure to call on me if I can ever be of help to you or Christina."

"You don't owe me anything, Father. It's a privilege to share in your ministry to our parish. Thank you."

"Be sure to call me when you get home. I want to know that you're safe."

"I will, Father. Stay safe and warm yourself."

It was nearly an hour later—after 10 p.m.—when Sean called Father T to let him know he arrived home safely. "I had to stop and help another car get out of a snow drift, but all's well that ends well. I'm home safely, and Christina is here with me. The university has canceled all classes for tomorrow, so I persuaded her to take the rest of the night off from studies. The children are all sound asleep, so we plan to sit quietly by the fire."

"Good night, Sean. And thank you."

Following a quick call to his cousin Vince to let him know he made it home OK, Father T retired for the night. He was exhausted, and sore from trudging through the snow, but he knew better than to complain about it to the Sacred Heart. "Lord only knows what he'll ask me to do next time he hears me bellyaching!"

DAY TWO
TUESDAY MORNING

Father T woke up at 5 a.m.—his usual time—and made coffee. The snow had stopped falling, but looking out the window he could tell that the streets and the church parking lot were a real mess.

The local TV weather forecast was for sunny skies but with bitterly cold, subzero temperatures (a high of only -4°F) throughout the day, overnight and for several days to come. Schools, churches, government offices, many businesses and every civic organization imaginable were closed. Except, of course, the homeless shelters and food pantries, which were all operating at full capacity.

After saying his morning prayers, Father T bundled up and headed over to the school building. Weekday Masses were always celebrated in the chapel, a former classroom that Father T converted to sacred space in order to reduce heating and air conditioning costs in the church which was much too large for the dozen or so people who regularly attended daily Mass.

"I don't expect anyone to come this morning," Father T said to himself. "It's too dangerous." More than once he had admonished his faithful daily Mass attendees saying, "Please don't put yourselves in harm's way. Our Lord will understand if you can't make it to Mass once in a while!"

But they were a stubborn lot—not unlike their pastor—and most of them showed up no matter what. This morning was no exception. Slowly but surely 10 of the 12 regulars walked through the back door of the school building, shook themselves off, and climbed the stairs to the former second-floor classroom that had served as a daily Mass chapel for more than 30 years.

"What's the matter with you people?" Father T asked with a wry smile before he said the opening prayer. "Joe and Rosemary are the only ones with any sense"

"But they're in Florida," one of the ladies responded.

"I know," said the priest, still smiling. "The Lord be with you."

After Mass, Father T had a second cup of coffee with two slices of toast. Instead of reading the newspaper in the kitchen (which wasn't delivered that morning anyway because of the snow), he watched the TV news upstairs in his sitting room. The weather was the "breaking news" that morning, which meant that the same bad news was reported over and over again until Father T could hardly stand it. Just as he reached for the remote to turn off the TV, he noticed a news item scrolled across the bottom of his screen. The enigmatic message read, "Missing girl attended St. Ambrose School. Police suspect foul play."

"Missing girl!" Father T exclaimed. "St. Ambrose School! Foul play! What the heck is that about?"

St. Ambrose was the Italian parish. It was Father T's first assignment as a young priest, and it was now his cousin's parish. If he ever retired from St. Roch, his plan was to go and live at St. Ambrose to help Msgr. Cugino.

"Who is this missing girl?" he asked out loud. "And why don't I know about this?

He grabbed his cell phone from his shirt pocket and speed dialed his cousin. "Vinnie," he shouted into his cousin's voice mail. "It's me. What's this about a missing girl and foul play? Call me!"

Not content to wait for his cousin's return phone call, Father T called Linda, his secretary, at home. In spite of her protests the day before, Father T had sent her home early and demanded that she not return until the weather broke. (He had done the same for his principal, Larry, and his maintenance man, Sam.) Linda was a member of St. Ambrose Parish. If there was any talk about a missing girl from the neighborhood, Linda would hear it.

"Linda, this is Father. I just saw on the TV that a girl from St. Ambrose School is missing. Have you heard anything about this?"

"No, Father. I haven't. But let me make some calls. I'll see what I can find out."

"Thank you, Linda. There's something strange going on here. I can feel it."

Father T switched channels several times hoping to learn more about the missing girl, but all he could find were stories about the polar vortex. The local weatherman was explaining (for the hundredth time!) that "a polar vortex is a large pocket of very cold air, typically the coldest air in the Northern Hemisphere, which sits over the polar region during the winter season." He went on to say that for some unknown reason this frigid air found its way into Canada and the United States when the polar vortex was pushed farther south. "And right now," the overly eager weatherman was saying, "it is sitting over southern Canada and the northern Plains, the Midwest and northeastern portions of the United States with no end in sight!".

More than 25,000 people were without power in the metro area—and many more in the county. Hundreds of cars had been abandoned on city streets, and all of the interstates and bridges had been closed by order of the governor. People were being warned to stay home and not attempt to go out.

"If you're not properly dressed," the mayor was saying on every channel, "just 10 minutes of exposure to this extreme cold can kill you."

"Jesus, Mary and Joseph!" the priest exclaimed. "What is this world coming to?"

Returning to his original news channel (the one that promised "fair and balanced" reporting), Father T watched for new information about the missing girl, but all he found were lists of school closings and more dire warnings from the mayor and governor.

When his cell phone began to vibrate in his shirt pocket, Father T turned off the television and looked at his caller ID. It was his niece Anna.

"Yes, Anna. How are you? Is your family OK? What about Aunt Anne?"

"We're all fine, Uncle Sal, including Aunt Anne. Her caregiver isn't happy she won't be relieved any time soon, but where could she go anyway? I called to see how you are, Uncle Sal. Do you have power? Is the rectory safe and warm?"

"Yes, Anna. We haven't lost any power, and everything seems to be working fine. I haven't been over to the church yet today, but I know the rectory and school building are holding up well."

"Do you have enough food, Uncle Sal?"

"Are you kidding? You know that I have enough meat-balls and red sauce in the freezer to feed an army."

"Man doesn't live by meatballs alone, Father. Do you have any lettuce, fruit or vegetables?"

"Yes. I went to Schnucks grocery store the day before yesterday. I was hoping to have Vinnie, Mike and John over for supper tonight. It looks like I'll be eating alone. Thank God for the homemade vegetable soup my former parishioner at St. Ambrose made for me!"

"Just be safe, Uncle Sal."

"I'll be fine. ... Say, Anna, have you heard anything about a girl from St. Ambrose who's missing? I saw a banner on a TV newscast, but it didn't give much information, and I haven't been able to get in touch with Vinnie."

"I'm sorry, Uncle Sal. I haven't heard anything about it. Why don't you call your parishioner who works at the newspaper? She'll have access to the police reports."

"Good idea. I'll give her a call. Thank you."

"Ciao, Uncle Sal. Be safe!"

Father T reached for the parish directory, but before he could look up the number, his cell phone began to vibrate in his hand. It was his cousin Vinnie.

"Where have you been, Vincenzo?"

"I was outside helping the guys from our men's club shovel snow in front of the church."

"Good Lord, Vinnie. You'll have a heart attack."

"The guys did most of the work, Sal. I mainly offered them moral support—and heavy doses of de-icing salt for good measure."

"What do you know about the reports that a girl from your school is missing? On the news they said something about foul play.

"Little Theresa Baglione has been missing since yesterday morning. At first everyone thought her father had taken her. Chris and Lisa are separated now, and there have been lots of arguments over custody. Chris lost his job a couple of months ago, and he's way behind in child support. Lisa told him he can't see Theresa again until he pays up."

"I hate it when children become victims of their parents'

insane behavior!"

"I agree, Sal. But I talked to Captain Ricci earlier this morning, and he says Chris is no longer a suspect. He's been doing some day labor for a construction company, and the foreman confirmed that he was on the job site working when Theresa disappeared."

"I know Lisa's family from the old neighborhood," Father T said. Her parents and grandparents were pillars of the Italian-American community and faithful supporters of the Church. I only met the Baglione boy once or twice at funerals for members of Lisa's family, but he seemed nice enough. I don't think he's from the neighborhood."

"He's from Chicago," Msgr. Cugino said. "He and Lisa met when he was studying at the university. He never graduated. When Lisa became pregnant with Theresa, Chris quit school to marry her and support the family. Now they're separated, and Chris is unemployed. So much for the American dream!"

"But who would kidnap their little girl, Vinnie? And why? Do the police have any leads?"

"Not yet. Once they determined that it wasn't the father, they put out an Amber Alert and called in the FBI. But in this weather no one is getting very far—literally—so until there's a ransom request or some other break in the case, there's not much anyone can do."

"Good Lord, Vinnie. This is just awful. How could these kids pay any ransom? It's insanity. Please keep me informed and let me know if there's anything I can do."

"Just pray to the Sacred Heart. Ask him to keep little Theresa safe. I'd hate to think what would happen to an 8-year-old girl who was left outside in this weather."

"I will, Vinnie. I surely will."

DAY TWO
TUESDAY AFTERNOON

For lunch, Father T had homemade vegetable soup and bread sticks with sesame seeds that he brought home with him from the Osteria, one of three restaurants operated by his good friends, the Norcini brothers. Afterward, he went over to the church to make sure there was no damage from the snow and ice. (Some men from the parish had cleared a path for him from the back steps of rectory to the church's rear entrance. They also made sure the ice was thoroughly covered with sand and salt.) Fortunately, everything checked out OK in the church. The boiler had been replaced just a few years earlier, and although Father T deliberately kept the thermostat set at a low temperature (60 degrees), there were no freezing pipes and no damage to the roof.

The missing girl was on the priest's mind. Things just weren't adding up. If her father was not to blame, who was? And why? And why would anyone think they could get ransom money from those young people Lisa and Chris? Father T was sadly aware of the presence of evil in our world, and, even more sadly, of the horrible things done to children. It made him furious to think of that little girl in the hands of someone (or a group of people) who would do her harm.

"When I first learned that some of my brother priests were guilty of horrible crimes against children," Father T used to say, "I couldn't believe it. I never imagined anything like that went on—anywhere—let alone at the hands of priests. In the neighborhood I grew up in, that kind of thing was never tolerated. The men in our community knew how to handle those kinds of people. End of story! The Sicilian in me wants to see child abusers (no matter who they are or where we find them) hanged from a lamp-post in the heart of downtown for everyone to see! But I also believe that everyone deserves mercy and God's forgiveness—provided we make sure they can never, ever, hurt a child again!"

Returning to the rectory, Father T went upstairs to his sitting room. It was too early to watch the afternoon news, so he simply sat in his easy chair watching the fire and saying intermittent prayers to the Sacred Heart and the Blessed Mother to intercede for little Theresa Baglione and keep her safe from all harm.

The warmth of the fire, and the unusually quiet rectory, caused the nearly 83-year-old priest to nod off. He dreamed of family members who had long since died and of more recent losses—his brother Dominic who died suddenly three years earlier at the age of 90 and his sister Jenny who passed away recently at the age of 92. He saw them all—the entire Turiddu family in much younger days—gathered around the kitchen table eating his sister Phil's cooking and laughing at his older brothers' stories about the "pazzi Americani" who came into the family's pecan factory without having the slightest idea what they were ordering or how much it cost. They often said it would have been very easy to cheat these crazy Americans, but the integrity of the Turiddu family would never permit it.

Father T woke when his cell phone began to vibrate in his shirt pocket. He recognized the number. It was his secretary, Linda, calling from home.

"Father, I'm sorry it took me so long to get back to you,

but it took me a while to find out anything. I had no trouble getting ahold of people because everyone is at home due to the weather, but no one had much to tell me."

"What did you find out, Linda? Monsignor Cugino says that Theresa Baglione is missing and all they know for sure is that her father is not responsible."

"I heard that too, Father. Apparently she was last seen when school was dismissed early due to the bad weather. I guess things were pretty chaotic at school yesterday, and no one noticed who Theresa went home with. The woman who usually takes her home couldn't get off work early, so one of the other mothers was asked to take her place. She says she never saw the little girl and, so, assumed Theresa went home with her mother or father."

"Monsignor Cugino and Sister Joella, the principal, will not be happy to hear about this. I know they have a system for making sure that every child is accounted for at the time of dismissal—even when the weather is bad."

"I agree, Father. It's a bad situation."

"Did you learn anything else, Linda?"

"No, Father. I'm sorry."

"That's OK, Linda. I appreciate your efforts. Between you and Monsignor Cugino, I have a lot more information than I did when I first saw the notice about a missing girl from St. Ambrose School on TV this morning. I wonder why the police suspect foul play?"

"I can't help you there, Father. The neighborhood grapevine is really quiet today."

Father T thanked his secretary. She was invaluable to him—loyal, trustworthy and extremely competent. Many pastors employed several people who served as members of the parish staff. Father T only had Linda, but she did the work of a dozen people and wouldn't have had it any other way!

◆ ◆ ◆

Theresa Baglione huddled in a corner of the abandoned factory building just three blocks from St. Ambrose Parish and School. In the old days, long before Theresa was born, hundreds of people from the neighborhood worked here making kitchen appliances. They didn't have cars. They walked to work. Many were uneducated, but as long as the factory remained open, it provided them with steady work close to their homes and families.

Now the old factory building sat empty—an eyesore that was no good to anyone. The neighborhood association which Father T helped form when he was an associate pastor at St. Ambrose in the 1960s refused to accept proposals for any use of the property that would devalue the neighborhood. Unfortunately, the owners refused to make the kind of investments that would be required to develop the property in productive ways that would add value to the local community. As a result, the large building sat empty year after year.

Fortunately for Theresa, the owners were required by their insurance company to heat the building just enough to prevent serious damage. Every 5 minutes, several large electric heaters blasted hot air into the factory. The result was enough to keep the pipes from freezing. It also prevented the 8-year-old little girl, who was curled up in a corner underneath one of the space heaters, from freezing to death.

Theresa was alive—no small miracle in the awful weather that everyone now called "the polar vortex." In the confusion surrounding the unexpected early dismissal of school, Theresa had decided to walk home. She didn't live far from the parish, or from the old factory, but in the whiteout that came suddenly during the extremely cold journey from school to her house, Theresa got completely turned around and could not find her way. After many wrong turns, she found herself at one of the factory's side doors. Pulling with all her strength, Theresa was able to open the door just wide enough to crawl inside to relative safety. But after 24 hours in this abandoned old building, she was hungry, thirsty and really scared.

◆   ◆   ◆

Monsignor Vincent Cugino took his pastoral responsibilities very seriously. Although he was nearly 20 years younger than his older cousin, Father T, he was still an "old school" priest, especially when it came to his duties as pastor. A whole lot of changes had taken place since his ordination in 1976, and like most of the priests of his generation, he had adapted fairly well. But there were some things he refused to let go of. Like his older cousin, being "on call" for parishioners who were sick or dying was sacrosanct. So was his responsibility for the children and youth of the parish, especially the children who attended St. Ambrose School.

"How could this happen?" Msgr. Cugino asked himself. "We're really careful about student dismissal. No child is ever allowed to leave with a stranger!"

Msgr. Cugino was pacing the hallway between his office and the rectory's kitchen. He was waiting for a return call from Captain Ricci at police headquarters, and he was just too nervous to sit at his desk by the phone.

There was a pot of homemade vegetable soup simmering on the stove. (It was made by the same parishioner who made soup for Father T. Both had enough to feed them for a month!) On the kitchen counter was a loaf of fresh-baked bread from the Italian bakery down the street. The bakery's owner, a long-time parishioner, brought Msgr. Cugino several loaves that morning. "No one will be buying any baked goods this morning," he said. "I don't want it to be wasted, Father, and I don't want you to starve to death." But Msgr. Cugino didn't feel like eating. He kept thinking about little Theresa. "Where can she be?" he asked out loud. "Please God, keep her safe!"

Normally, the St. Ambrose rectory was a busy place with lots of parishioners in and out all day. Now, except for the sounds of the pastor's pacing (and talking to himself) it was strangely quiet. No parish business would be conducted today. The small parish staff had all gone home the day before. Msgr. Cugino had checked on each of them, and he was thankful that they, and their families, were all safe. He had also checked on his 92-year-old mother who lived by herself in a small apartment nearby. "Stay in today, Mother, and don't try to go anywhere. If you need something, give me a call."

"Where would I go in this blizzard, Vincent?" Mrs. Cugino said. "I've lived in this city for 92 years, and I've never seen a winter like this one."

When the rectory phone rang, it startled the priest. He ran from the kitchen to his office to answer it. "What news do you have for me, Captain?" he asked impulsively.

"This isn't the captain, Vince. It's John." Msgr. John Dutzow was the pastor of a nearby city parish and a good friend. He had joined Msgr. Cugino on several of Father T's adventures over the years.

"I'm sorry, John. I was expecting a call from Captain Ricci. We're trying to locate a missing child."

"Sal told me about the little girl, Vince. I'm very sorry. Is there anything I can do to help?"

For many years, Msgr. Dutzow had served as chaplain to the city fire department. He was very familiar with search and rescue operations—especially involving missing children.

"There's not much any of us can do, John, except pray," Msgr. Cugino said. "As you know, in almost any other circumstance we'd have teams of rescue workers and parishioners combing the neighborhood streets searching for Theresa. Every inch of this parish would be covered. But there's no way that can happen now with temperatures well below zero and snow so thick you can't see what's right in front of your face. It's driving me crazy. We can't just sit here and do nothing!"

"I know, Vince. I can't imagine a worse time to search for a missing child. Please let me know if there's anything we can do."

"Thank you, John. Pray that the snow stops soon and that we find Theresa unharmed."

DAY TWO.
TUESDAY EVENING.

Theresa had wrapped herself in the winter coat her mother bought for her at Christmas time—just before her father lost his job. It was a wool coat with a hood, but it wasn't enough to keep her from shivering uncontrollably as she lay on the factory's hard concrete floor. It was getting dark and the thought of spending another night alone in this dreadful place was overwhelming to her. Based on the previous night's experience, she knew that after nightfall the factory would be so dark that she could not see anything. All night long, Theresa had listened to strange, scary sounds as she sobbed and shivered. The thought of repeating that terrible experience was more than she could stand, and once again she began to cry.

She had done some exploring earlier in the day. Old machinery, trash and years of accumulated dust were all she found. When she tried to open the small side door—the one she had found open the previous afternoon when she was lost in the storm—she quickly realized that there was no where she could go. A blast of really cold, arctic air, followed by more snow than she had ever seen before, told her she was trapped. Theresa was only 8, but she was smart enough to know that, no matter how frightening the factory was, this was the safest place to be. Still she sobbed and shivered, wondering when her mommy or daddy would come to get her.

◆　◆　◆

Father T was as impatient as his younger cousin. He had spent most of the afternoon on his cell phone calling his contacts in the police department and the FBI. Everything was a dead end. There was no ransom demand, and no clues as to the whereabouts of this little girl from the Italian neighborhood who had now been missing for approximately 30 hours in the worst winter storm anyone could remember. During all 58 of his years as a priest, Father T had never lost a child. Never!

His cell phone vibrated in his shirt pocket. The caller ID told him it was Msgr. Cugino.

"Any news, Vinnie?"

"Nothing. I just talked to Captain Ricci. He said he spoke to you earlier and there are no new developments. He told me that he and the FBI now believe this is not a kidnapping."

"I think that's right," Father T said. "But it could still be an abduction by someone who wants that poor child for reasons other than money."

"I know, Sal. It makes me sick to even think of it."

"What should we do, Vinnie? We can't just sit on our hands and do nothing."

"There's nothing we can do tonight, Sal, except bombard the Sacred Heart with prayers for Theresa's safety. But first thing tomorrow morning—blizzard or no blizzard—we're going to search the neighborhood. I have a dozen young men from the parish who have agreed to go out with me tomorrow morning. We'll take turns driving the streets in SUVs and snow mobiles and with the help of St. Ambrose, St. Anthony, and St. Jude, we'll find our lost little girl!"

"You can count on my prayers to the Sacred Heart, Vince. Nonstop. I even raised my voice and shouted at him. I was afraid he couldn't hear me over the howling wind and snow."

"He hears us, Sal. That's why we have to keep at it and not lose heart. You taught me that many years ago."

"I've been praying especially for Theresa's poor parents who must be totally overwhelmed with guilt and fear," Father T said.

"The good news is that they are together again and are doing the best they can to support one another in this awful time. The ladies of the parish have been taking turns visiting them and bringing them food. How any of them has managed to get through the unplowed streets on a day like this is truly amazing!"

"Sacred Heart of Jesus, have mercy on the Baglione family," Father T prayed. "And please—please—please—help us find their little girl unharmed!"

DAY THREE
WEDNESDAY MORNING

Father T celebrated Mass in the chapel at 7:15 a.m. He shared with his parishioners his concerns about little Theresa, and he asked them all to join him in praying for the intercession of the Blessed Mother, St. Roch and St. Ambrose.

"We have to find her," the priest repeated several times. "We have to bring her back safely to her poor parents and family!"

Before going to bed the night before, Father had once again called his young parishioner, Sean McEnroy, to ask another favor.

"Sean, I have to go to St. Ambrose tomorrow morning no matter what. A little girl from the parish is missing, and I need to help my cousin and his parishioners search for her. Is there any way you can take me there?"

"Absolutely, Father, and I'll help with the search."

"What about Christina and your children?"

"As you know, Father, school has been cancelled for all of them for the rest of the week. They're not going anywhere. We have plenty of food and water, and so far we haven't lost power. I'll check with Christina, but I know she'll want me to help find Theresa. We've been watching the story on the TV news."

"You're a good friend, Sean. Thank you."

Sean was among the small group of faithful Mass goers that morning. As soon as Mass was finished, he and Father T drove south across Forest Park to the city's south side and the Italian neighborhood. The whiteout had ended, but the fierce winds continued to blow snow across the roads impairing visibility. The combination of ice and snow made driving treacherous. Sean's SUV managed to move slowly but steadily, through the ruts which were nothing but packed ice and drifted snow. As they drove, Father T thanked the Sacred Heart for his young companion. There was no way that the priest's little Mazda could have made this trip given these awful conditions.

The two men didn't talk much. Sean kept his eyes on the road ahead, and Father T tried to concentrate on what they should do to find little Theresa.

"Either she was taken by someone or she's lost her way," he said out loud. "If she was taken, we'll have to rely on the authorities to find her and get her back. But if she's lost in the neighborhood, you, Vinnie and I, with the help of St. Ambrose parishioners, are her best hope. We know the territory. We know every inch of that neighborhood, and we won't rest until she's home again safe and sound!"

Father T's cell phone buzzed in his shirt pocket, and it took him a while to reach inside his coat, vest and sweater to retrieve it. It was Msgr. Cugino.

"Are you coming? The men are all here now, and we're ready to begin."

"We're just crossing the railroad tracks. We'll be there in 5 minutes."

"OK, but we can't wait much longer. We have to find Theresa before it's too late."

"I know, Vinnie. Sean and I will be there as soon as we can."

The railroad tracks that Father T and his companion

were crossing played a big part in the priest's efforts to "save the Italian neighborhood" in the days when the Interstate highway was being built. The original plans did not include an overpass, and, as a result, the neighborhood was inaccessible to emergency vehicles several times a day when long trains stopped all traffic.

Father T had lobbied hard to get the overpass approved, but it wasn't until the highway construction workers, who had been befriended by the Italian-American community, sided with the neighbors and stopped working that plans for the overpass were finally approved. That was the second time Father T earned the title "*il salvatore della città*, (the savior of the city)."

When they arrived at St. Ambrose, Father T pointed out to Sean that the statue of Italian immigrants in front the Church, which he had commissioned many years earlier, had been cleared of all accumulated snow. "The people of this parish are proud of their heritage," he said. "They take especially good care of their parish and school, and they're very good to their priests! I only wish my cousin had more help. This is such a busy place—especially with all the extra weddings and funerals for former parishioners who want to come "home" for all the important moments in their lives. One full-time priest just isn't enough for a busy parish like St. Ambrose!"

Msgr. Cugino and more than 20 men and women were waiting for them in the newly renovated parish hall. A handful of off-duty police officers joined them, but nearly all city police were on-duty that day trying to deal with all the traffic and emergency-rescue problems created by the polar vortex.

"We've divided the neighborhood into quadrants," Msgr. Cugino said. "Everyone has been assigned to a quadrant, and we've given the searchers strict instructions. They are not to be outside in the open air for more than 10 minutes before returning to a warm building or heated car for another 10 minutes. We don't need anyone collapsing—or worse—because of the extreme cold."

"Sean and I will go with you, Vinnie. We can take Sean's SUV if you'd like. It does a great job in the frozen ruts and deep snow, and it will keep us warm."

"OK, Sal, but I want you to stay in the vehicle. I know you're healthier than most men half your age, but we can't afford to take any chances in this subzero weather. Do you understand me?"

"Yes, Father. I understand you, but I really don't know why you're making such a fuss about me. Let's just get going. That poor little girl needs our help."

The five search teams headed out into different sections of the Italian neighborhood looking for Theresa. It was not an easy task. Snow was piled up along both sides of the narrow streets, and there were abandoned cars everywhere making driving even more difficult. When the searchers' vehicles stopped, and everyone but the driver (who was required to stay with the vehicle and keep it warm) got out to search on foot, the going was very slow and very difficult.

"What are we looking for?" Sean asked before he and Msgr. Cugino got out of their vehicle. (Although he was not the driver, Father T was told to stay in the SUV and keep it running and warm while his cousin and his young parishioner searched for signs of the little girl.)

"We're looking for any sign that Theresa might have been here—or any indication that something unusual happened in this part of the neighborhood. I know it's a long shot, but what else can we do?"

The searchers saw plenty of trees and shrubbery bent

over with ice and snow. They also saw fellow parishioners waving to them from windows covered by frost. Large icicles hung dangerously from the gutters. Under other circumstances, the ice and snow would have been pictur-esque, but no one was taking pictures of romantic snow scenes. It was just too cold!

"Have you seen a little girl anywhere?" Msgr. Cugino would call out when a neighbor opened his or her front door to greet him, but no one had seen anything. The way the snow had fallen the day Theresa went missing, with the blinding wind and piercing cold, it would have been a miracle if anyone had seen anything, let alone a little girl trying to pass along the street in a blizzard.

After 10 minutes, Msgr. Cugino and Sean returned to their vehicle disappointed.

"I don't ever remember being this cold," the Monsignor said to his older cousin. "I hope you're praying to the Sacred Heart. We need some divine intervention here."

"We're not far from the Baglione home," Father T said. "Let's go and see how Chris and Lisa are holding up."

"OK, Sal. I talked to Chris this morning. He wanted to join us for the search, but the FBI advised him to stay near the phone on the off chance this is a kidnapping. He said that Lisa is scared to death."

"All the more reason to go and see them."

"Agreed, but there's one more street we have to travel to get there. Sean and I will see what we can find out there. If Theresa decided to walk home yesterday, she would more than likely come this way."

"Unless she cut through the alley," Father T said. "That's the route I would take if I wanted to walk from St. Ambrose to her house."

"Yes, but the alleys are completely inaccessible" Msgr.

Cugino said. "No one plows the alleys—ever, so in this kind of storm the snow just piles up until it melts!"

"Jesus, Mary and Joseph," Father T exclaimed. "Please keep this poor child safe and warm!"

Sean followed Msgr. Cugino's direction, guiding his Chevy Suburban through the ice-packed ruts and the snow drifts. When they reached the next street, he pulled the SUV as close to the snow piled on the right so that he and Msgr. Cugino could exit from the left. (Father T was riding shotgun in the front of the vehicle.)

As the two men trudged through the street slowly, and with much difficulty, looking for anything out of the ordinary, Father T continued his conversation with the Sacred Heart of Jesus. "What are we missing, Lord? Send us a clue—anything that will lead us in the right direction."

The Sacred Heart was silent. All the priest could hear was the SUV's idling engine and the sound of the heater blowing warm air.

Suddenly, Father T felt his cell phone vibrating in his shirt pocket underneath all the layers of warm clothes he was wearing. In his haste, he fumbled the phone and dropped it between his seat and the passenger door next to him. The only way to retrieve it was to climb over the center console, kneel on the driver's seat, stretch out over the passenger seat and use both of his hands to search for his cell phone.

"It's a good thing I'm in good health and agile," the priest mumbled to himself (and to the Sacred Heart). "There are some advantages to sticking with an old-style flip phone instead of upgrading to something with a lot more bells and whistles. I'm going to stick with what I have—if I ever find it!"

Father T eventually did find it—right between the seat

and the door—and when he checked his voicemail he saw that Mary Castelucci had left him a message.

"Mother passed away this morning, Father T. She was very peaceful. Thank you again for braving that awful storm and anointing her. It meant so much to her—and to me. Call me when you can, Father, so we can discuss her funeral arrangements. I sure hope the weather improves in a few days. Most of her friends are elderly. There's no way we can give her a proper Mass and burial the way things are now."

"*Requiescat in pace,*" Father T prayed as he closed his phone. "May Andrea rest in peace. She's been a very good friend to me ever since I was first assigned to St. Roch. I will miss her."

Msgr. Cugino and Sean returned to the SUV empty-handed and discouraged. "This is hopeless," Father T's cousin told him. "We can't see anything, and we can hardly walk. How can we conduct a proper search in this weather?"

"Let's go see Chris and Lisa," Father T said. "Maybe we'll catch a break."

It was past noon when Father T and Msgr. Cugino arrived at the Baglione home, which was just three short blocks southeast of St. Ambrose—and 2 blocks west of the abandoned factory where Theresa had taken refuge unbeknownst to her parents or her pastor and the neighborhood search party! Sean McEnroy remained in the SUV to keep it warm while Father T and Msgr. Cugino went inside. Chris and Lisa Baglione were seated in the living room of their modest home with two FBI agents and members of Lisa's family who were long-time parishioners at St. Ambrose.

"We're doing everything we can to find Theresa," Msgr. Cugino said as her parents greeted them. "We're searching every inch of the neighborhood. If she's out there, we'll find her."

"Thank you, Monsignor, but it's so cold. How could she survive?" asked the girl's grief-stricken mother.

"The Sacred Heart is with her, Lisa" Father T replied. "We've been praying to him nonstop since we heard the news. I trust in him implicitly. He's never let me down yet."

"There's been no ransom call and no indication she's been abducted," Theresa's father said. "We know the weather is a serious obstacle, but we really should be out there looking for her. We think she is lost not kidnapped."

"A search team from St. Ambrose with the help of city police officers is out there right now looking for her," Msgr. Cugino said. "We just stopped by to see how you're doing."

"Did Theresa ever walk home from school?" Father T asked.

"Never by herself," Lisa answered. "But once in a while, in good weather, I would pick her up after school and we'd walk home together."

"What route did you take?" Father T asked.

"We'd take Wilson for 2 blocks and then cut through the alley."

"How would you go if the alley were blocked?"

Lisa thought for a moment. "It only happened once, but the alley was blocked by a garbage truck one day, so we continued east on Wilson past the old factory and then circled back.

"The factory!" Father T exclaimed. "Let's go, Vincenzo. We need to check it out now!"

"I'm coming with you," Chris said. "I don't believe anyone will call, but if they do the agents here will tell Lisa what to do."

The three men joined Sean in his Chevy Suburban and headed east toward the abandoned factory.

"Can you go any faster?" Father T asked his young parishioner from his front row seat.

"For the love of God, Sal," Msgr. Cugino said. "It's a miracle we can make any progress at all in this mess. We'll get there in God's good time."

"I'm sorry, Sean. My young cousin is right. Let's get there safely—but as soon as possible!"

"Do you really think Theresa is at the factory?" Chris asked Father T.

"She's a smart little girl. If she headed home all by herself in that awful storm yesterday, and found the alley impassable, she might very well head toward the factory. I'm counting on the Sacred Heart to lead us to her there."

"I sure hope you're right, Father. I've been praying to St. Ambrose. I promised him I'd be a much better husband and father if Theresa comes home safely."

◆ ◆ ◆

Theresa huddled in the corner. She had been there since the previous night and had only gotten up once that morning to use the bathroom she found the day before. It was not clean, but it was usable. The space heaters kept the pipes from freezing, so she had water to drink from the bathroom sink. But poor Theresa was very hungry, and weak, and really frightened.

The wind made loud noises that competed with the periodic roaring of the space heaters. Still, she thought she heard someone calling her name. It was very faint, and seemed far away. Could it be her daddy? Surely Mommy and Daddy were looking for her. Theresa knew they would find her. But when?

"Hurry, Daddy," she whispered softly to herself. "Please hurry."

When the space heaters cut off, she was sure she heard someone calling her name.

"Theresa, where are you?" cried several voices. She was sure one of them was her daddy's.

"Here, Daddy!" she called as loudly as she could, but in her weakened state her voice didn't carry beyond the factory walls. "Here, Daddy. I'm here!"

The door that Theresa had used to get into the factory the day before was now blocked by several feet of frozen snow and ice. Chris Baglione, Sean McEnroy and Msgr. Cugino each took turns pulling as hard as they could, but they were unable to force the door open. Father T watched from the

SUV. He was not at all pleased when his cousin told him to stay in the vehicle, but he acquiesced—for now.

"We'll have to break a window and climb in," Msgr. Cugino said.

"The windows are all boarded up," Sean replied. "Will we be able to break them down?"

"Only one way to find out," the priest said as he swung a large snow shovel at the nearest ground floor window. The glass shattered but the thick plywood board covering the window from the inside didn't budge." Msgr. Cugino tried two more times with no success.

"This is not ordinary plywood. It's heavy-duty hard-wood. It's very tough, especially when it's nailed to the window frame," Chris said. "We'll need more than a snow shovel to break through it."

Theresa heard the glass break and the pounding Msgr. Cugino gave the boarded window. She ran to the place where the noise was loudest and cried out, "I'm here, Daddy. I'm here. Please come get me!"

But the wind was still howling, and there was no way an 8-year-old's voice could overcome it. Theresa stood by the window and called out for what seemed like forever until her voice failed her and she could barely produce a hoarse whisper. Finally, she just sat down on the concrete floor and cried.

Father T watched as the three younger men attempted to break down the boarded window. He was now absolutely convinced the little girl was in there, and he pleaded with the Sacred Heart to show them the way to get inside!

When Msgr. Cugino, Sean and Chris returned to the SUV, having spent at least twice as much time in the sub-zero weather as they should have, they were discouraged and shaking from the cold.

"We'll have to call the fire department's rescue squad," Msgr. Cugino said. They have the right equipment to force open the doors and windows. We don't."

"What about the loading dock?" Father T asked. "Could Sean's truck ram one of those doors and break it down?

"Not a chance, Father" Chris said. "I've seen those docks. They're elevated so that large trucks can back up to load or unload. Sean's SUV isn't nearly tall enough to ram one of those doors."

"Call the fire department, Vinnie," said Father T. "But in the meantime, let's keep trying. I'm going to go out and look around while you guys warm up."

"That's not a good idea, Sal," his cousin said.

"Nonsense, Father. All I'm going to do is look around. I'll be back in 10 minutes when it's time for you three to go out again."

The nearly 83-year-old priest adjusted his layers of clothing and put on the thick gloves he purchased 25 years ago for his annual ski trip to Colorado with his cousin and two other priests. It was never this cold on any of his ski trips. "This is insanity!" he muttered to himself. "We never have winters like this. Never!"

Father T walked along the side of the factory in the opposite direction from where his colleagues had broken the window. His plan was to walk for 5 minutes and then turn around and head back. After a few minutes of very slow going ("trudging" was the right word for it), Father T noticed a small shed-like structure with a flat roof attached to the main building. Above it was a small window that was not boarded. As he came closer, the priest saw that the frozen snow was piled high enough all around the shed to allow someone who was light and agile to climb onto the roof and, perhaps, to open and climb through the window.

Father T knew that he should go back to the SUV and tell the others, but he didn't. "I've always been a man of action," he said to himself. "Sacred Heart of Jesus, please be with me," he prayed out loud as he scampered up the snow drift, slipping and sliding as he struggled to find places to hold onto, and finally hoisted himself onto the roof of the shed. He could feel the shed creaking. "Dear God, I hope this roof is strong enough to hold my weight on top of all this heavy ice and snow!"

The window was higher up than it had seemed from the ground. When Father T stood under it he realized that he would need to grab ahold of the windowsill and pull himself up in order to climb through the window. That meant he had no choice but to break the window. Even if the window was unlocked, he was not tall enough to open it. His only choice was to break it and then pull himself up and through it.

As Father T stood looking at the window, he shuddered and sighed deeply. He was becoming numb from the bitter cold. "It's now or never," he said to himself as he grabbed a clump of frozen snow—an ice ball really—from the roof of the shed and hurled it at the window. The glass shattered, but the opening was not large enough for even a thin man like Father T to climb through. It took two more ice balls hurled at the remaining glass to open it wide enough for Father T to get in, but even so there were sharp edges around the frame making it dangerous (at best) for the elderly priest to attempt to pull himself up and through the now-open window.

"Thank God for these thick leather gloves," he said to himself. "Sacred Heart of Jesus, help me out here," he cried out loud as he reached up, grabbed the windowsill and pulled himself up and through the window into the old factory. As he hit the floor face first, Father T quickly rolled over on his back. He stayed that way for a few minutes and then stood up to assess the damage. His gloves were torn, and his hands were sore, but he wasn't bleeding. The shoulder where he once tore a rotator cuff ached, but he could tell that there was no real damage.

"Thank you, Jesus. Now please help me find that little girl."

◆　◆　◆

Msgr. Cugino had been paying close attention to the time since his older cousin left the vehicle promising to return in 10 minutes. Nearly twice that amount of time had passed, and he was worried.

"What has he gotten into now?" he asked himself, not wanting to worry Sean or Chris. All three were waiting for the city fire department's rescue team, and their patience had just about run out.

"I'm going to see what's keeping Monsignor Turiddu," his cousin said. "You guys wait here for the rescue team."

"With all due respect," Chris responded. "If there's any chance my daughter is in that building, I'm not going to sit here any longer."

"OK, Chris. We'll let Sean wait for the fire department. Let's go look for Father T. He headed this way. We'll follow his tracks in the snow."

About 5 minutes later, the fire department's rescue team arrived.

"I'm so glad you're here," Sean said as he got out of his SUV to greet them. "We think the missing girl is inside, but the doors are either locked or frozen shut, and the windows are boarded."

"Are you here by yourself?" one of the rescue team members asked.

"No, there are four of us—two priests, the little girl's father and me. The others went around the building, that way, trying to find a way to get inside."

"OK. Unfortunately, the department could only spare two of us with all the other problems created by this weather. Let's get in the building first to see if we can find the little girl, then we'll look for the others."

Msgr. Cugino was right. The boarded window was no match for fire department's equipment. Two blows from the modern day battering ram held by the two professionals knocked the heavy plywood to the ground, and all three climbed through the now-open window into the factory.

There, sitting on the concrete floor, were two figures huddled together—an elderly Sicilian-American priest and an 8-year-old girl still shaking from the cold and from fear but very happy to be held by her rescuer, the man her family and neighbors knew as *il salvatore della città*.

One of the rescue workers wrapped Theresa in a warm blanket. The other said, "Now we need to find the others."

"Others?" Father T asked.

"He means Monsignor Cugino and Chris," Sean replied. They went to look for you. They're probably circling the building."

"Daddy!" Theresa cried as her father and their pastor climbed through the now-open window. Chris was beside himself, crying tears of joy.

"Your tracks led us to the broken window above the shed," Msgr. Cugino said to Father T, but we couldn't believe you would actually climb up there and go through it. I half expected to find you crumbled and broken on the factory floor!"

"The Sacred Heart was with me, Father. I was not worried. I trusted him to help me find Theresa, and as usual he didn't let me down."

"Let's get this little girl home," one of the rescue workers said. "She needs her mother."

"And some homemade soup," her father added. "Our friends from St. Ambrose brought us enough food to feed the whole neighborhood. You're all welcome to join us. This is a time for real celebration!"

Chris and Theresa went home with the rescue team while Father T, Msgr. Cugino and Sean followed. Msgr. Cugino used his cell phone to contact his parishioners and call off the search. "Meet us at the Baglione house," he said. "Chris and Theresa want to thank us and offer us some lunch featuring hot soup and bread. We won't stay long."

When Sean's SUV pulled up in front of the Baglione home, Father T recognized another black SUV which had been meticulously cleared of the last two days' accumulated ice and snow.

"That's John's car," he said to his cousin. "What's he doing here? I bet one of his old cronies from the fire department called him."

In fact, former Fire Department Chaplain Msgr. John Dutzow was called as soon as Msgr. Cugino requested the rescue team. He was on his way to the old factory from his nearby parish when he heard his scanner radio report that Theresa had been found and was about to be taken home by her rescuers, so he drove to straight to the Baglione home. He was waiting with Lisa, her family and the FBI agents (who were packing up their phone-call-tracing equipment) when the rescue team arrived with Theresa.

The reunion was a joyful one with lots of hugs and kisses (and hot soup) for Theresa. As the little house filled up with neighbors and members of the search teams, Lisa took her daughter to her bedroom to let her rest.

"I knew Daddy would come for me," Theresa told her mother. "I prayed to Jesus and Mother Mary, and they sent Daddy to find me."

"Lots of people helped Daddy find you. They were angels of mercy sent by Jesus to help us."

"I know, Mommy. My guardian angel stayed with me when I was in the building so I wouldn't be alone. Do you know what he looks like?"

"What does he look like, sweetheart?"

"He's old and thin and has gray hair—just like Father T."

"Go to sleep now, darling. When you wake up, everything will be OK."

Father T finished his evening prayers by the warm fireplace in his sitting room. He was especially grateful to the Sacred Heart, and he said so. "I trusted in you, Lord, and you didn't let me down. Grazie!"

The weather was less severe now. The snow had stopped, giving the highway workers a chance to clear the main streets, but the temperature was still dangerously below zero. Father T knew it would take several days—perhaps a week—before things started to return to normal. He checked on his sister and family. All were safe and warm. He called his friends. Everyone was where he or she was supposed to be and out of harm's way.

The news reports disturbed the elderly priest. There was never any good news. Why didn't the media tell the stories of heroism and hope that were part of every tragedy? Little Theresa's rescue was mentioned on the evening news, but very little was said about the parishioners from St. Ambrose who risked their own lives to search for her.

"I know, Lord. I should focus on what's good and be grateful. It's just that so much goodness goes unnoticed while every problem is magnified a hundred times!"

Just as Father T was about to change the channel, another news report caught his attention. In Washington, D.C., a good friend from his days as an urban planner was being indicted on charges of espionage.

"This is insanity!" Father T shouted at his television set. "John Urbansky is the most loyal American I know.

He would never betray his country!"

The priest grabbed his cell phone in his shirt pocket and searched for his friend's number. When he punched-in the number, he reached his friend's voice mail.

"John, this is Father T. Call me. I can't believe what I'm hearing on the news. Let me know how I can help."

Turning back to the TV, Father T searched the cable news networks to see if he could get more information. According to the reports, John Urbansky was suspected of collecting sensitive data under the guise of city planning and then sharing it with foreign nations and perhaps even terrorist groups. He had been arrested at his home earlier that day and was being held by federal agents for questioning and possible arraignment the next day.

"Jesus, Mary and Joseph!" Father T exclaimed. "When it rains, it pours! It just never stops. Sacred Heart of Jesus, what do we do now?"

Father T's cell phone vibrated in his shirt pocket. The caller ID told him it was his niece Anna Dominica.

"Have you seen the news reports, Uncle Sal? It looks like your friend John Urbansky is in serious trouble."

"Yes, Anna. I'm sick about it. It has to be a mistake. John would never do anything to hurt our country. He's a true patriot."

"What can I do to help, Uncle Sal?"

"Nothing yet, Anna," Father T said. "In the morning, I'll call my friend Bob Taormina at the FBI here in the city and ask him to check with his connections in Washington. We'll find out what's going on first and then take whatever action is necessary. I may be almost 83 years old, but I refuse to just sit back and let my good friend be falsely accused."

"You're sure he didn't do it, Uncle Sal?"

"Absolutely sure, Anna. Absolutely!"

"OK. Keep me posted, and let me know what I can do."

"Good night, Anna. And stay inside tomorrow. It's not getting any warmer!"

"You, too, Uncle Sal. Good night."

After a few more phone calls—to his cousin Vinnie and his friends Father Mike and Msgr. Dutzow—Father T went to bed. His sleep was fitful as he worried about his friend now held under lock and key in the nation's capital. He couldn't help remembering their times together many years ago as they worked to help urban communities like Father T's beloved Italian neighborhood overcome the effects of racism, white flight and the misguided policies of "urban renewal." John Urbansky was a brilliant strategist who knew the ins and outs of the Washington bureaucracy. Father T relied on him for useful information and for guidance on how to lawfully circumvent the powers-that-be. He trusted John implicitly, but he worried about him, too.

"Sacred Heart of Jesus," he prayed as he eventually dropped off into an uneasy sleep. "Take care of John and his family. Please."

DAY FOUR
THURSDAY MORNING

The rectory telephone woke Father T at 4 a.m. "What now?" the priest said to himself as he fumbled with the light switch and picked up the phone.

"Hello. St. Roch Catholic Church," he said.

"Father, help us, please. Our electricity is out; the pipes are frozen, and it's getting dangerously cold here in the house."

"Who is this?"

"We're your neighbors, the Chumleys. We're not Catholic, but we live just a few streets away on Delmar."

"Have you called 911?"

"We didn't think of that."

"I'm terribly sorry, Mrs. Chumley, but I have no way of helping you. Call 911 and tell them what your situation is. If you don't get help, call me back, and I'll do my best to find someone who can help you."

"Thank you, Father."

Father T hung up the phone and turned off the light, but he didn't sleep. He was not used to feeling so helpless when neighbors (Catholic or not) asked for his assistance. Besides, John Urbansky was on his mind. What kind of data could an urban planner share with foreign governments? The whole thing was absurd.

He lay in bed until around 4:30 and then decided to get up and say his morning prayers. As he opened his well-worn breviary, a favorite prayer of St. Ambrose fell out on the floor. It was a meditation on the Gospel image of the Good Shepherd who leaves his flock in search on one lost sheep.

> Seek me, Lord; I need you.
> Seek me, find me, lift me up, carry me.
> You are an expert at finding what you search for;
> and when you have found the stray, you stoop down,
> lift him up, and place him on your own shoulders.
> To you, he is an object of love, not an object of
> revulsion;
> it is no irksome task to you to bring justice to the
> human race.
> Come then, Lord, I have gone astray,
> but I still hold on to the hope of healing.
> Come, Lord; none but you can bring back your
> erring sheep.

"Sacred Heart of Jesus, I do need you," Father T prayed. "Help my friend John Urbansky. Help all those who are suffering from the cold today, especially my neighbors, the Chumleys. Bring justice to the innocent. And grant peace to all who are oppressed. Amen."

Downstairs in the kitchen, he made a pot of coffee. It was still more than an hour before he would celebrate the 7:15 a.m. Mass in the chapel, and Father T was hungry. Not wanting to break the one-hour fast before he received communion, the priest quickly ate a piece of toast with jam.

He could hear the wind howling in the parking lot outside his kitchen door. When he looked out the window, he saw the snow swirling and drifting. No new snow was falling, but the lot would still be treacherous due to the blowing snow and ice underneath. He wished he could call his faithful daily Mass attendees and tell them to stay home, but he knew they wouldn't listen. When Mass began, the majority of them would be seated in their usual places in the chapel. They always were—no matter what!

During Mass, Father T prayed for John Urbansky—not by name but as "a friend in special need of our prayers." The little congregation of faithful parishioners could tell that their pastor was disturbed. They suspected—correctly—that he was frustrated by his inability to help this friend in special need.

At 8 a.m. precisely, Father T was in his office in the rectory looking up the telephone number of the FBI's local agent in charge, Robert Taormina. Thirty seconds later the agent answered the phone and was greeted by a familiar voice.

"Roberto, this is Father T. I saw on the news last night that my very good friend John Urbansky has been arrested in Washington, D.C., on some trumped-up charge. What can you tell me about this? More importantly, what can we do about it?"

"I saw the same news reports you did, Father. That's all I know. Give me some time, and I'll see what I can find out."

"Of course, Roberto, but please hurry. I don't want John to suffer this humiliation any longer than is absolutely necessary!"

"I understand, Father. I promise I'll get to the bottom of this—and fast."

"You're a good man, Roberto. Please give my best regards to your mother. She was a dear friend of our family, and we spent many hours together sitting at the kitchen table in the old neighborhood. My sisters were her very best friends."

"I know, Father. She'll be very pleased to hear that I talked to you today. She'll be 93 in a few months, but she's still going strong! I'll give her your love."

The priest went up to his study to watch the cable news for any new developments in his friend's case. Unfortunately, they were still reporting the same information over and over again. Frustrated, he switched to the Italian channel where a game show host was leading two contestants in an effort to win prizes by some kind of guessing game.

"Not today," Father T said to himself. "I can put up with this nonsense some days because it helps me practice my Italian. But not today!"

The rectory was too quiet for Father T's peace of mind. St. Roch was not a bustling parish like St. Ambrose. In the Italian parish, there was always something—several things—happening day and night. St. Roch was a quieter parish community. But even at St. Roch it was rare to have absolutely nothing going on, no one calling the rectory, and no one in the house but himself.

Cabin fever is what they call it when the walls start to close in on you, and you're desperate to get out—no matter how horrible the weather! Father T was definitely suffering from cabin fever, and he found himself torn between a strong desire to get out of the rectory and the equally strong conviction that the smartest thing to do was to stay inside and not have to face the awful weather caused by this strange polar vortex.

Around 10 a.m., the rectory phone rang breaking the strange silence.

"It's Bob Taormina, Father. I have some news."

"Thank God, Roberto. What's the story?"

"Well, it seems that your friend John was working on a

government contract that involved gathering data via satellite. That required him to have special clearance, and it also gave him access to classified information."

"What kind of information?"

"That's not clear, Father. My sources don't have access to this information. All we know is that Mr. Urbansky is suspected of selling this classified information (whatever it is) to the Chinese."

"The Chinese! Jesus, Mary and Joseph! That's the stupidest thing I've ever heard. John Urbansky would never get involved in selling secrets to the Chinese—or anyone else. On my mother's grave, I swear to you, Roberto, there's no way this can be true."

"I hear you, Father. But that's what I've been told. I'm very sorry I can't tell you more."

"It's not your fault, Roberto. Do you know if he has legal counsel? I want to make sure he has the best possible representation."

"I'll find out for you, Father."

"Please do, Roberto. Then call me back—as soon as you can. This is insanity! John's wife, Marge, and their children must be beside themselves with worry."

Father T put the rectory phone down and then immediately picked it his cell phone. The night before he had called John Urbansky's cell and left a message. Now he searched his contacts for John's home phone number. He dialed and a woman answered.

"Marge, this is Father T. I just heard the terrible news about John. How is he—and how are you and the children?"

"This isn't Marge, Father. I'm her sister Helen. I've been screening calls to keep Marge from having to talk to reporters. Marge is upstairs lying down. If you can wait just a minute, I'll call her. I'm sure she'll want to talk with you."

"Thank you, Helen, but tell her I'll understand if she doesn't want to be disturbed. She can call me later if that's best for her."

A few minutes passed, but to the anxious priest it seemed like an hour.

"Hello, Father. This is Marge." Her voice was weak, and Father T could tell she had been crying.

"How are you holding up, Marge? What can I do to help you—and John?"

"It's been a nightmare, Father. They came to the house unannounced with a warrant for John's arrest and another one to search the house. It was awful. John was taken away in handcuffs, and they tore our house apart. Two of our grandchildren were with us, and they were scared to death. I've never seen such a mess. If it wasn't for Helen, we'd still have everything we own scattered all over the floor."

"Did you call an attorney?"

"Yes. That was the first thing I did when they took John away. I called Joe Thiele, an old family friend. He's trying to get in to see John, but so far the government isn't letting anyone near him. They say it's a matter of national security. Can you believe it, Father? You know as well as I do that John would never do anything to harm our country. This has to be a huge mistake. Why can't they see that, Father?"

"I don't know, Marge, but I've turned this over to the Sacred Heart. He's never let me down yet. And I'm talking to my friends in the FBI. One way or another, we'll get to the bottom of this. John will come home to you soon. I promise. How are your grandchildren doing?"

"Their mother came to get them. You remember Betty, Father. She was just a little girl when you first visited us here. Now she's married and has two daughters of her own, ages 8 and 10."

"Marge, you tell Betty that we'll get her dad released if it's the last thing I do. This whole thing is insanity. End of story!"

"You are such a good friend, Father. Thank you."

"Goodbye, Marge. And God bless you."

THURSDAY AFTERNOON

After another bowl of homemade soup and a slice of fresh bread, Father T went to his office to read his email. The small office was unpretentious and overflowing with letters, articles and other documents. The walls were covered with photographs of family members and friends dating back more than 50 years. A large portrait of the priest's mother shared space with framed posters and other memorabilia from Father T's days as an urban planner.

Just outside the office, the rectory's front hallway contained hundreds of different images of the Blessed Virgin Mary. Father T called it his "Marian wall" and every time he was given a new image of Christ's mother, he made sure it found a prominent position on the wall. Father T was known to pace up and down the hallway conversing with Mary and asking for her intercession in especially troubling cases. John Urbansky's current situation definitely fit that description—so much so, in fact, that if anyone else had been in the St. Roch rectory that afternoon, they would have sworn they overheard a three-way conversation involving the Sacred Heart of Jesus, his Blessed Mother and Monsignor Salvatore E. Turiddu.

"John Urbansky does not deserve this treatment, Lord. Yes, I know that we can't know everything about our friends, but in John's case I can speak with absolute certainty!"

"Holy Mother of God, give him consolation and hope. I understand that you will stay close to Marge and her family. Thank you, Blessed Mother."

"But what are we waiting for? You know I have no patience. None. Please, Sacred Heart, help me."

"Mary, Seat of Wisdom, show me a way to be helpful. I can't stand being cooped up in this rectory when my good friend needs help!"

When he finished pacing, Father T went back to the kitchen and looked out the window to the parking lot. He tried to assess whether he would be able to de-ice his car and make it out of the lot.

"But where would I go even if I could get away? The airport is closed and in this weather it would take days to get to D.C. on a bus or on Amtrak."

"I surrender, Lord. Your will be done. But please help John and Marge—not for my sake but for my good friend and his family!"

There were no important emails and, of course, no street mail, so Father T turned off his computer and went back upstairs to his sitting room. As he climbed the familiar back stairs, he felt a numbness in his right leg that made it difficult for him to lift it up and take the next step. He stopped at the landing to rest. After a minute or so, he felt better and continued up to his sitting room.

Seated in front of the fireplace, Father T opened his breviary and turned to the Evening Prayer—Vespers—for that day. It was only mid-afternoon, but the priest hoped that saying his prayers would help him shake off his restlessness. As was his custom, he first checked the Ordo, a book in which the archdiocese listed the anniversary dates of priests who have died). Most of Father T's classmates pre-deceased him. The rest were either retired or infirm.

It was rare for a diocesan priest to be active—serving as a full-time pastor—at nearly 83, and Father T was keenly aware that the Lord had blessed him with good health and the desire to remain active in his priestly ministry. Still, he was sometimes very tired. In those moments, he thought about all those who had gone before him. They were good men—some better priests than others—but all of them had given their lives to serving God's people.

"Help me, Sacred Heart of Jesus, to use the gift of good health for the service of your people. Help me to be a good shepherd, like you, who leaves his comfortable place in order to search for the one who is lost."

The priest's eyelids drooped and he slept softly in his chair. He dreamed of Msgr. Adrian, "The Boss," who was his pastor at the Italian parish. The Boss was not an Italian-American but he spoke the language fluently after many years of study and then teaching in Rome. Most of what Father T knew about Church politics he had learned from The Boss who was fond of saying, "*Genuit porci porcos* (Pigs beget pigs)," which was his way of dismissing all bureaucrats—whether in the Church or in society.

As he dreamed, Father T thought he heard The Boss speaking to him in Italian, but he couldn't make out the words. He was sure it had something to do with John Urbansky, and he was very frustrated that he couldn't understand what his old mentor was telling him. "*Genuit porci porcos* " was all he remembered when he woke up. He wasn't sure that's what The Boss was saying in the dream, but he was convinced that it meant something important.

"What was The Boss trying to tell me?" he asked himself. "And what does his old saying about Church bureaucrats have to do with John's situation now?"

Father T took his cell phone from his shirt pocket and

called his good friend Father Mike Belcamp.

"It's me, Mike. What are you up to?"

"This crazy weather is causing real problems for our Catholic Cemeteries staff. No burials are possible, of course, and there's no way we can keep the roads in the cemeteries clear. We had to shut the gates and keep people away (the few who wanted to visit family members' graves), and I'm the one who has to answer the angry phone calls. You know how you'd feel, Sal, if you couldn't visit your mother on her anniversary."

"I hate this damn weather, Mike. It's cruel to everyone."

"I have a question," Father T said. "I'm sure you've seen the news reports about John Urbansky. I talked to Marge earlier and she's beside herself. Bob Taormina says that the government thinks he's been selling hacked satellite data to the Chinese."

"Impossible. John Urbansky is one of the most honest men I know. Where do they get this nonsense?"

"I don't know, Mike. I wish I did. Can I ask you a question that may seem strange?"

"This whole situation is strange, Sal. Go ahead."

"Well, I fell asleep in my chair after reading my breviary and I dreamed about The Boss. He was trying to tell me something. At first I thought he was speaking Italian, but the more I think about it, the more I think it was Latin. Do you remember his telling us that pigs come from pigs? What would that have to do with John Urbansky?"

"I don't know, Sal, unless it has something to do with the bureaucrats in Washington who have accused him of stealing government secrets."

"That has to be it, Mike. Of course! John is a victim of unscrupulous thugs in Washington who have falsely accused him of something—probably to cover-up their own wrongdoing!"

"Now slow down, Sal. We're just speculating about an idea that was buried in your subconscious. We have no proof of anything—and no reason to level accusations against anyone."

"I know, Mike. But I feel it deep in my Sicilian bones. There's something very wrong here, and I'm going to get to the bottom of it—even if I have to travel to Washington by dog sled!"

"Don't get the dogs out just yet. Keep talking to Bob Taormina. He's a good man. He'll help us if anyone can."

"OK, Mike. It's time for me to check in with him anyway. I'll let you know how it goes."

Father T placed a call to his friend at the local FBI headquarters but got his voicemail.

"Roberto, this is Father T. Call me please. I have a question for you. ."

THURSDAY EVENING

John Urbansky was very depressed. He had never been in prison before—even as a visitor! And although the federal detention center he was in was a lot nicer place than most local, state or even federal facilities, he was still a prisoner.

"What have I done to deserve this? Surely this is just a stupid mistake that will be all over—soon! I'm not sure how much of this I can stand."

He still couldn't believe that the FBI had come to his home in suburban Maryland with two warrants—one for his arrest and the other to search his home.

"Tell me what you're looking for," he had said to the agents. "If I have it, I'll gladly give it to you."

But the agents simply proceeded to tear the place apart looking for whatever it was they thought he might have that would shed light on their suspicions.

"Can you tell me what I'm accused of doing?" John asked as he was escorted to a government vehicle. Apart from reading him his rights, the arresting agents were silent.

Even when they interrogated him at the detention center, they gave no real indication what they thought he had done. Many of their questions were easy to answer. When he could, he responded simply—and always truthfully. But sometimes he really had no clue what they were asking him about.

"I don't understand," and "I don't know what you want from me" were his frequent responses especially when they asked about satellite codes or data that had nothing to do with his research as a city planner. He was equally confused by questions about people they assumed he knew who were completely unknown to him.

"I really don't know any of these people," John said. "If I did, I would tell you. I have absolutely nothing to hide."

◆ ◆ ◆

Father T didn't have much of an appetite, but his internal clock told him it was time to think about supper. He knew he had meatballs and sauce in the basement refrigerator, and there was plenty of pasta in the kitchen cupboard and lettuce in the refrigerator. But cooking for one person had never been his idea of a good use of his time.

At exactly 6 p.m., Father T's cell phone began to vibrate. It was his cousin Vince.

"What are you planning for supper, Sal?" Monsignor Cugino asked.

"Nothing. You know I can't stand cooking for one."

"Good. John and I are on our way. The Chinese restaurant on DeBaliviere is open, and we're going to stop there for take-out."

"Why are you coming all the way over here on this awful night? Stay home. I'll be fine."

"We're afraid you'll go stir crazy and try to drive your little car somewhere. We'd rather bring you Chinese food now than end up pulling you out of a snowdrift later. Stay put and we'll be there in a half an hour."

"OK, Vincenzo, but this really isn't necessary."

Father T watched the evening news—first the local channel and then the national news. He especially liked what the syndicated columnist Charles Krauthammer had to say about the ongoing nonsense in Washington.

"I should call Dr. Krauthammer," Father T said out loud to his TV set. "He can help me figure out what the heck is happening to John!"

Charles Krauthammer had earned Father T's respect because his views were always clear and carefully considered. Even if Father T didn't always agree with him, he respected him. After a swimming accident paralyzed him when he was a first-year medical student, he continued his medical studies at Harvard and graduated with his class, earning his M.D. in 1975. He became a chief resident in psychiatry at the Massachusetts General Hospital. In 1984, he became board certified in psychiatry. His brief tenure as a eminently successful practicing psychiatrist was followed by a career in journalism that earned him the reputation of being one of the most highly regarded political commentators in the United States. When Dr. Krauthammer spoke, Father T listened.

"That's more than I can say for our local newspaper," he always said. "There's nothing 'fair and balanced' about that rag—especially when it comes to the Catholic Church!"

Most of the news coverage that evening—local and national—concerned the polar vortex and the havoc being wreaked on most of the continental United States. That frustrated Father T. He was tired of hearing about this awful weather, and he was eager for more news about his good friend John Urbansky.

Close to 7 p.m., the back doorbell rang, and Father T hurried to the kitchen to let his friends in. "It's much too cold to be standing at the back door," he said to himself as he fumbled with the keys and unlocked the door. "Besides we don't want our supper to get cold."

Msgr. Cugino and Msgr. Dutzow hurried into the rectory kitchen as soon as Father T opened the door.

"Man it's cold out there," Msgr. Dutzow said. "I don't

ever remember a winter like this—even when I was assigned to the country parish many years ago."

"My memory goes back a lot farther than yours, John," Father T said, "and I can assure you this is the worst winter ever. End of story!"

Stop talking about the cold," Msgr. Cugino said. "Let's have something to eat and drink that will warm us up."

Father T's appetite turned out to be larger than he thought it was earlier in the evening, but it was still no match for the boxes of Chinese food that his cousin and friend had ordered from the little Chinese restaurant on DeBaliviere Avenue.

"There's enough food left over to feed an entire village in Sicily," Father T said. "You guys take this home with you. There's no way I could eat it all even if I'm stuck here for the rest of the winter!"

"We'll divide it three ways," Msgr. Cugino said. "That way each one of us will have some leftovers to reheat tomorrow."

The three priests' conversation during dinner had been mainly chit-chat. Once the dishes were hand washed and placed in the dish rack, the three priests went into the front sitting room for an after dinner drink and some serious conversation.

"Sal, on the way over tonight Vince told me what you found out about John Urbansky," Msgr. Dutzow said. "None of this makes any sense. What can we do to help?"

"Thank you, John. I've spoken with Marge and with our local FBI director Bob Taormina. So far there's not much to go on. Prayers for John and his family are the main thing we can do right now. When the weather breaks, I may make a trip to Washington to see if I can shake things up there. God knows the knuckleheads in the federal government need it!"

"Who stands to gain from putting John Urbansky away?"

Msgr. Dutzow asked.

"That's exactly what I plan to ask Bob Taormina when he calls me back. I have a hunch this has something to do with D.C. bureaucrats protecting their turf."

"Do you think John accidently uncovered something that someone doesn't want him to know?" Msgr. Cugino asked.

"I have no idea," Father T said. "But there's absolutely no question in my mind that John Urbansky has been falsely accused by someone!"

"With all due respect, Sal," his younger cousin said. "city planning is not the first thing you think of when international espionage is involved."

"I don't know, Vince. I can think of several reasons why foreign governments or terrorists groups would want to get their hands on confidential information about our nation's cities—especially New York, Washington, Boston or Philadelphia. But all of this is beside the point. John Urbansky is innocent. End of story."

DAY FIVE
FRIDAY MORNING

All of the regulars (except the two snowbirds who were in Florida) were present for Father T's morning Mass. The parking lot had been plowed at 5 a.m.—just as the pastor was beginning his morning prayers. After Mass the priest scraped the ice from his car and started the engine. The weather forecast was for clear skies, no precipitation and temperatures only in the single digits. "Insanity," Father T said to the young TV meteorologist who was the bearer of this morning's bad news. "I don't ever remember a winter this cold!"

Traffic reports on the early morning news said that major roads and highways were now passable but that motorists should beware of "black ice." The city's side streets remained treacherous, so Father T didn't plan to go anywhere. He just wanted to make sure that his car was drivable "in case of emergency."

At 8 a.m. the priest was back in his rectory kitchen warming up with another cup of coffee and toasting a slice of Italian bread with sesame seeds. When his cell phone began to vibrate in his shirt pocket, he saw that it was Linda, the parish secretary.

"Don't even think about it," Father T said before his secretary could say a word. "I'm fine, and I don't need you to come in to work today. The roads are still awful and the temperature is even worse. Stay where you are."

"I know, Father, but I have so much work to do."

"It will wait, Linda. What's most important to me is that you are safe and warm."

"OK, Father. But I'll be there tomorrow no matter what."

"Tomorrow is Saturday. I don't want to see you until Monday. Understood?"

"All right Father, but you stay safe and warm yourself. Any word about John Urbansky?"

"No, Linda, but I plan to call Bob Taormina shortly. I have to do something about this nonsense—now! If only I weren't trapped inside this rectory. It's driving me crazy."

"I'm praying to the Sacred Heart and the Blessed Mother, Father, especially for Marge and her family."

"Thank you, Linda. Prayer is powerful. Thank you for reminding me. I'm hardwired for action, as you know, and I just can't stand be trapped in this rectory when a good friend needs my help."

"Patience, Father. The Sacred Heart never lets you down."

"Never!" Father T said. "Thank you for being such a good friend, Linda."

◆ ◆ ◆

John Urbansky had spent a sleepless night on the extremely hard cot in his cell. He was worried about Marge and about his future.

"Thank God I have my faith," he said to the bare walls that were closing in on him. "I'm not sure I could bear this if I didn't believe that a merciful God was watching over me and my family. *Deus providebit*. God will provide."

A slight tap on the door, followed by the sound of a key

being inserted in the lock, demanded his full attention.

"You have a visitor," said one of the prison guards.

It was his attorney, Joe Thiele. John was very happy to see him, but he didn't like the somber look on his face.

"How are you, John? Are they treating you OK here?"

"I'm OK, Joe, but please tell me when I can get out of here. I have no idea what any of this is about. Marge has to be worried to death!"

"Marge is fine, John. You know how strong she is. She's praying hard that this misunderstanding will be cleared up and you'll be home soon."

"What can you tell me about 'this misunderstanding,' Joe. I really can't figure it out. Based on the questions they're asking me, my guess is they think I stole something—a database or confidential files. I swear to God, Joe, I have done nothing wrong."

"I believe you, John, but sad to say, in these kinds of cases, you're guilty until we can prove your innocence. Can you give me any idea what the government is looking for or why they suspect you?"

"I really have no idea. I'm a city planner. I don't have access to top-secret information, and I certainly wouldn't sell confidential information to anyone, if I had it!"

"OK, John. I'm working hard to get to the bottom of this. They can't just keep you here indefinitely without filing charges, and when they do, I'll do my best to get you out on bail. In the meantime, don't give up hope. Our justice system isn't perfect, but it's a whole lot better than most other countries'."

"Thank you, Joe. Marge and I are very grateful."

"By the way, Marge told me that your good friend Monsignor Salvatore Turiddu called. She asked me to tell you that Father T is working on your case. What does that mean?"

"It means he's enlisted the Sacred Heart and a team of family members and friends in an effort to help me. Father T is Sicilian-American. Last year he and several friends and family members rescued a high-ranking Vatican official from terrorists. The year before, they foiled a plot to blow up abortion clinics here in the states. This is great news, Joe. Father T is a powerful advocate—and a very good friend!"

"Well don't get too excited, John. The federal bureaucracy may turn out to be your friend's toughest case yet! Our best bet is to continue putting pressure on the government to either charge you or release you."

◆ ◆ ◆

Father T's cell phone vibrated in his shirt pocket. It was Bob Taormina calling from the FBI building downtown. He was returning Father T's early morning call.

"Roberto, what can you tell me?"

"Not a lot, Father. The CIA is involved, and they're keeping things very close to the vest. I've reached out to a good friend in the agency, and he's promised to do some investigating for me off the record. I hope to hear from him later today or tomorrow."

"Bob, this can't continue. John is an innocent man, a patriot. Something is very wrong here, and we need to get to the bottom of it—fast. Would it help if I found a way to go to Washington and talk to the people in charge? I'm sure I can convince them that this is all a big mistake."

"Well, Father, even if you were able to get out of here, I'm not sure you can land in Washington. You know how they're paralyzed by bad weather. The entire government shuts down. That's one of our problems right now. There's hardly anyone working during the storms caused by the polar vortex. It's impossible to get any information."

"I'm storming heaven, Bob. But it's driving me crazy. There must be something else I can do. Will you let me know as soon as your CIA friend calls you? I really hope he can help."

"You know I will, Father. Ciao."

"Goodbye, Roberto. I'll be waiting for your call."

FRIDAY AFTERNOON

Father T was weary and stressed out. He didn't feel well, so he only ate a small portion of the soup he had warmed for lunch. Upstairs in his sitting room, he tried to read but he discovered his eyes wouldn't focus. Soon he was asleep.

More than an hour later, the rectory phone rang. The priest heard it ringing but it sounded like it was far away, in another part of the 100-year-old building. Gradually he shook off the drowsiness that covered him like a blanket, and as he became more aware, the ringing got louder and closer.

"St. Roch Parish. How can I help you?" said Father T.

"Sal, it's me, Vince. I've been calling your cell phone, but you didn't answer. I was worried about you."

"I took a nap, Vincenzo. I guess I didn't feel it vibrating."

"Are you OK?"

"Yes, I'm just a little tired. And I'm worried—and frustrated—about John Urbansky. I really wish I could go to Washington to help him."

"I know, Sal. You're not used to being idle. Listen, Mike and I are coming over around six tonight. We're going to pick you up and take you to the Osteria for dinner."

"That's crazy, Vinnie. Stay home."

"No, we've already made our plans. The Norcini brothers are expecting us. This weather has been really hard on their business. We want to show our support."

"I guess it would be good to get out of here. I have a bad case of cabin fever. Lord, how I hate this awful weather!"

"We'll see you at six, Sal. In the meantime, take it easy. See if there's a soccer match on the Italian channel. You need something to take your mind off this weather."

"What I need is to get John Urbansky out of federal custody and home to his family!"

"I know, Sal. I know."

There was no soccer match on the Italian channel so Father T watched an Italian soap opera. "These goofy programs are all the same," he said to himself, "but they help me practice my Italian."

"I wish Vinnie spoke the language," Father T often said, "but he's one generation removed from it. His parents didn't speak Italian at home the way mine did. That makes a big difference."

The afternoon wore on, and the priest had no energy even for his prayers. Something was wrong with him, but he brushed it off. "Maybe I'm coming down with the flu," he thought. "It's definitely flu season!"

FRIDAY EVENING

By the time his cousin Msgr. Cugino and his friend Father Mike arrived, Father T was barely able to walk down the stairs and open the kitchen door.

"What's wrong, Sal?" Father Mike asked. "You look awful."

"I think I caught a flu bug. Maybe you guys should go to dinner by yourselves."

"Why are you dragging your left leg and leaning to one side?" Msgr. Cugino asked. Did something happen? Did you fall?"

"I'm fine, Vinnie," but he didn't sound fine. His voice was slurred. "I'm just tired, and as I told you, I think I'm coming down with something."

"I don't believe it, Sal," his younger cousin said. Where are your hat and coat? We're going to the emergency room to have them check you out."

"I agree with Vince," Father Mike said. "It's better to be safe than sorry. If it is just the flu, they'll give you something for it."

"I don't have the energy to fight with you, but I think this is unnecessary. I'll be fine once I have a good night's sleep."

Father T slept in his cousin's car on the way to the hospital. The roads were icy, so Msgr. Cugino couldn't make the kind of time he would have liked. Father Mike used his cell phone to call ahead and alert the emergency room staff and the hospital administrator, who was an old friend, that Father T was on his way.

Father T was no stranger to this or any of the other hospitals in the city. He made his rounds weekly—sometime daily—visiting and anointing the sick and the dying. He couldn't recall the last time he was in the hospital as a patient. (It was probably when he broke his arm while skiing many years earlier.) The medical staff was ready with a wheelchair as soon as Msgr. Cugino pulled up at the entrance to the ER, and there was no delay in getting him in to see the doctor.

Tests confirmed that the nearly 83-year-old priest had had a slight stroke. The damage was minimal, just some weakening of his left leg and arm. In spite of the priest-patient's objections, the ER doctor checked with the neurologist on call and admitted him for overnight observation saying that if nothing changed, he could go home the next day. Msgr. Cugino and Father Mike supported the doctors' decision. They offered to stay overnight with him, but Father T wouldn't hear of it.

"If the two of you don't leave now and go home," he said as soon as he was settled in a private room, "I'm going to get dressed and go home myself. I don't need any babysitters. I know practically every nurse in this hospital. They'll take very good care of me. Just come back in the morning and take me home!"

Msgr. Cugino and Father Mike stopped at the Osteria where Father Mike had left his car. The Norcini brothers, Bart and Mike, took very good care of them. When they found out that Father T was in the hospital, they offered to take him some dinner, but Father Mike convinced them that what their friend really need was a good night's rest.

"Not easy to do," Mike Norcini said. "When I had my

heart surgery, they woke me up every hour to check my vitals. A hospital is no place to try to get some sleep!"

"We'll send some food to the rectory tomorrow," Bart said. "Father T will be hungry for a good Italian meal when he gets home!"

The two priests took turns calling Father T's family and friends. Father T had told them not make a big deal of this, but they knew that there were people who would be offended if they heard about it second-hand.

"How serious is this?" Father T's niece Anna asked Msgr. Cugino. "Be straight with me. I want the whole story."

"All indications are that this was a very slight stroke. The doctors believe he will recover fully in no time, but they're keeping him overnight as a precaution."

"Will he need physical therapy?" Anna asked.

"Probably, but it's too soon to say for sure how much damage was done. Thank God his mind is clear and his speech was only slightly affected."

Father Mike called Msgr. John Dutzow who had been having some health problems of his own. "I'll stop by the hospital in the morning after Mass," he said. "I have a couple of parishioners who are there, and it will be good to stop and see them. The crazy weather we've been having threw me off my regular schedule of hospital visits."

"Shouldn't someone call the archbishop, Father Mike asked?"

"My guess is that Sal will want to do that himself tomorrow morning," Msgr. Cugino said. "Let's wait and ask him what he wants."

Father T slept like a baby that night—undoubtedly due to the medication he was given. He dreamed he was watching his sister Phil cook his favorite meal, Pasta Turiddu, for supper. He could smell the aroma in his dreams. Bart was right. He would be hungry for a home-cooked Italian meal as soon as he got out of the hospital!

DAY SIX
SATURDAY MORNING

Robert Taormina was working overtime on John Urbansky's behalf in spite of the fact that it was not his case and he was located half a continent away from the nation's capital. He knew that Father T would not rest until his friend was cleared of all suspicion. He also had an intuition that something was very wrong with this case.

After several phone calls to former colleagues in the FBI's main office, the story was beginning to get clearer. The FBI believed that a terrorist group considered to be loosely affiliated with ISIS (not the Chinese!) had been collecting information about Washington D.C., including the location of underground tunnels and the placement of gas lines. Because John Urbansky had access to this information as a city planner, he was one of several people the bureau identified as suspects. When they began to look into him, the FBI field agents discovered what they thought were unusual communications between John and members of a Syrian family thought to have connections with a network of Mideast terrorists.

John Urbansky had not been arrested because there was insufficient evidence that he had committed a crime, but he was being held for questioning under provisions of the Patriot Act whose constitutionality even a veteran FBI agent like Bob Taormina questioned. "Charge him or let him go home to his family," the agent said to himself as he reviewed his notes.

Agent Taormina's initial call to the rectory at St. Roch went unanswered, so he tried Father T's cell phone. A groggy voice answered.

"Roberto, what can you tell me?"

"Good morning, Father. I hope I didn't wake you."

"Nonsense. I've been up for hours. I'm in the hospital—nothing serious, just a very mild stroke. I'm going home as soon as your pastor comes to get me. (He has the 8 o'clock Mass every day now because he has no assistant.) What have you found out about John Urbansky?"

"I've confirmed that they are questioning John about a Mideast terrorist group that somehow got possession of classified information that he has access to. No charges have been filed but he is being held without bond until a determination is made about his involvement in this case."

"Insanity!"

"I know how you feel, Father. I promise to keep you informed as things develop,"

"Thank you, Bob. Do you know whether John has been allowed to consult his attorney?"

"I was told that he has, Father. The attorney's name is Joe Thiele. He's an old friend of John's and he has an excellent reputation."

"Can you get me the attorney's phone number? I want to talk to him myself."

"Of course, Father. I'll look it up and call you back."

"Thank you, Bob. If I don't answer, just leave a message. Who knows what kind of tests they'll put me through before I can get out of here! Unlike poor John, I at least know for sure that I'll be having supper at home tonight."

"I hope you have a full recovery, Father. Please let me

know if there's anything I can do for you."

"Just help me get John Urbansky out of federal custody!"

"I'll do my best, Father. I promise."

Later that morning, Father T's doctor, a former parishioner from the Italian neighborhood and the son of one of the priest's best high school friends, paid him a visit.

"You're a very lucky man, Monsignor Turiddu. The damage caused by the stroke was minimal. Six weeks of physical therapy and you should have normal use of your left arm and leg. I'm prescribing medication that will greatly reduce the risk of another stroke, but you have work to do too. You need to relax and not take things so seriously. Anxiety is very bad for you, Father. You have to learn to let go of your troubles and place them in God's hands. Otherwise there's a good chance you'll wind up back in this hospital bed—or worse. Do you understand?"

"Yes, Doctor. From now on all my troubles will be handed over to the Sacred Heart. He's never failed me yet."

"OK then. I'll sign the discharge order, and you can go home."

"Good. Thank you. Monsignor Cugino is my ride. He's visiting some parishioners here in the hospital. We'll leave as soon as he's finished."

SATURDAY AFTERNOON

Father T was silent on the road home. His cousin could tell he had something on his mind.

"What are you thinking, Sal?"

"The doctor is right. I let myself get all tied up in knots over John Urbansky's situation. It's so hard for me to sit quietly and do nothing when a good friend needs my help."

"What John needs is for you to stay healthy. You're no good to him—or any of us—if you're all tied up in knots or in the hospital."

"I know, Vince. But it's hard."

"John, Mike and I have been talking. We're going to take turns spending the night with you at St. Roch until it's clear that you're OK on your own. John will stay with you tonight; then Mike and then me. End of story!"

"I won't argue with you, Vinnie. Truth be told, I welcome the company. But I'll be back on my feet in a couple of days. You'll see. I may be almost 83, but I have more stamina than pastors who are half my age!"

"What do you want to tell the archbishop?"

"I called him early this morning. He was just about to take his dogs for a walk. I assured him this is nothing serious, and he promised to keep me in his prayers."

"OK, Sal, but please don't try to do too much. John and Mike and I are here for you. Let us help you whenever we can."

"I'm grateful, Vincenzo. I really am."

When Father T and Msgr. Cugino arrived at the St. Roch rectory, Msgr. Dutzow and Father Mike were waiting for them.

"Are you hungry, Sal?" Father Mike asked. "The Norcini brothers gave us risotto, insalata caprese and veal cutlets. You can have it now or save it for later."

"Is there enough for all of us?" Father T asked.

"Of course."

"Then let's eat. You guys don't mind if I let you set the table. I'm still a little weak."

So the four priests ate a hearty meal and engaged in chit-chat at the dining room table. Father T ate more than he really wanted, but he was happy to be surrounded by his good friends.

After lunch, Father T said he wanted to take a nap. "I don't have to worry about the 4 o'clock Mass today," he said. "Msgr. White comes over from All Saints Parish every Saturday evening, and I take the two Masses on Sunday."

"Not tomorrow," Msgr. Dutzow said. "My Masses at St. Mary Magdalen are being handled by my senior associate. I'll say the two here at St. Roch."

"John, that's really not necessary. I'm strong enough to say Mass."

"Not tomorrow, Sal. You need to get your strength back. It's all been arranged, so don't argue. I'm staying here tonight and saying both Masses in the morning."

"OK, John. Thank you. But I have Andrea Castellucci's funeral on Monday morning. There's no way I'm going to miss that. Mary came to see me in the hospital, and we made all the arrangements."

"You're really something else," Msgr. Cugino said. "If we're not careful, you'll be on the next plane to

Washington with a scheme to liberate John Urbansky from the clutches of the federal government."

"Is the airport open yet? I just might do that."

SATURDAY EVENING

Father T's afternoon nap lasted several hours. By the time he woke up, the 4 p.m. Mass of Anticipation was well under way. As he looked out his bedroom window, he could see the cars arranged in rows that were bordered by large snow mounds. The winter sky was clear, but the wind was blowing and the snow was swirling through the parking lot and the side streets behind the church and rectory.

"What a week it's been! The worst weather in a century, a missing girl in the Italian neighborhood, this nonsense with John Urbansky and a mild stroke to boot! I've never seen anything like it."

Father T was on his cell phone talking to John Ford, his parish council president .

"Kathy and I never should have left the city on vacation," John said. "Here in Belize we have warm sunshine and absolutely no drama. Maybe you should come down here for your recovery, Father."

"You know better than that, John. I'd be bored to death."

"Well please be assured that Kathy and I are praying for you—and for John Urbansky and his family."

"Thank you, John. You're a good friend."

It was time for the evening news. Father T normally switched between local and national channels, but tonight he was hoping to learn more about his friend's situation.

Most of the evening's coverage was still focused on the polar vortex and its aftermath. Airports were beginning to reopen allowing thousands of stranded travelers to rebook their canceled flights and make their way home. Cities across the nation were digging out, clearing the main roads and praying that temperatures would gradually rise to normal winter levels. Cabin fever was becoming epidemic among the millions of people who had been confined to quarters, and according to the news media, the crime rate, which had dropped dramatically because of the severe weather, was slowly beginning its climb to PPV (pre-polar vortex) levels.

Toward the end of the broadcast, just before a commercial break, the program's host (a substitute "sitting in" for the regular anchor) announced that the closing segment, which featured a panel of three journalists, would discuss the case of John Urbansky, the city planner accused of espionage. Father T immediately increased the volume while calling out to Msgr. Dutzow who was saying his evening prayers in the guest room.

"John, come here. They're going to talk about John Urbansky on the news. I'm calling Vince and Mike to let them know."

Msgr. Dutzow joined his friend in the upstairs sitting room in front of the fire, the portrait of the Sacred Heart and the pastor's large screen TV.

"What's happening, Sal?"

"As soon as this silly commercial is finished, they're going to discuss John's case."

When the substitute host returned, he showed a news clip from the day before that recapped the story of John Urbansky's apprehension and the allegation that he had sold state secrets to a foreign government. No new information was provided, but the program's host invited panel members to comment.

George Will, a conservative writer and avid baseball fan, said that as far as he could tell there was no evidence to connect this honest and hard-working city planner to any crime.

"He's absolutely right!" Father T shouted. "There's no way John would commit this—or any other—crime. End of story!"

Kirsten Powers, a Democrat, said she wasn't so sure. The government must have some evidence or they wouldn't have detained him for questioning or obtained a search warrant for his home and office.

"Poppycock," Father T mumbled. "They can search all they want, and question him all day long. They won't find anything incriminating. It doesn't exist!"

Finally, Father T's favorite, Dr. Charles Krauthammer, spoke.

"Look, this is a ridiculous waste of time and money. I reviewed the case thoroughly. I even went back and researched Urbansky's history as a city planner. This is clearly an innocent man who's either been identified by mistake or is being set up as a patsy."

"Yes," Father cried. "He's being set up as a patsy! But why? And by whom?"

"That's the $64,000 question," Krauthammer was saying as if in response to the priest who had shouted this question to his flat-screen TV. "If I were Mr. Urbansky's attorney, I'd be asking myself who stands to gain from the prosecution of this innocent man."

"That's what I said to Bob Taormina," Father T said to Msgr. Dutzow (and the television panelists). "Something fishy is going on here, and I'm going to get to the bottom of it!"

"Not so fast, Sal," Msgr. Dutzow said. "Remember what the doctor told you. You can't afford to get too worked up about this kind of thing."

"I know, John. I have to turn it over to the Sacred Heart."

"Do you hear that, Lord?" Father T looked directly at the image of the Sacred Heart above his fireplace. "This is in your hands now. Please don't let us down. We have to find out who set up John Urbansky—and we need to find out now!"

When the evening news was finished, Msgr. Dutzow went back to the guest room to finish his evening prayers. Father T picked up his breviary, but he immediately set it down again. There was no way he could concentrate on printed words on a page. Instead, he softly recited prayers he learned as a child—many of them Marian prayers like the Memorare, the Regina Coeli, and, of course, the Hail Mary.

"Remember, O most gracious Virgin Mary," the priest repeated for the second or third time, when his cell phone began to vibrate in his shirt pocket. He wasn't familiar with the number, so he almost didn't answer it, but he recognized 202, the Washington, D.C, area code and was curious to see who might be calling him from the nation's capital.

"Hello. This is Father Turiddu."

"Good evening, Father. My name is Joe Thiele. I'm John Urbansky's friend and legal counsel. I have good news."

"Thank God you called, Mr. Thiele. What can you tell me?"

"John is being released tomorrow morning. The government has decided not to charge him. There simply isn't enough evidence."

"That's fabulous news, Mr. Thiele. I'm so happy for John and Marge and their family."

"We still have some work to do, Father. Although John isn't being charged, he's still under a cloud of suspicion until the investigation is completed and he is completely exonerated. That could take some time."

"The Sacred Heart is in charge, Mr. Thiele. He won't let us down."

"Thanks for all your prayers, Father. John and Marge were convinced that you would help them out of this jam. I see now that they were right."

"All I did was turn John's case over to the Sacred Heart and try to stay out of the way. If I'd done that sooner, John might be at home right now!"

"It's a pleasure talking with you, Father. I hope we have a chance to visit next time you're in town."

"I'd like that, Mr. Thiele, but I don't get to Washington much anymore. I'm almost 83 years old, and my days as a political organizer and urban planner are well behind me. I mainly take care of my parish and my family now. God bless you, Sir. Please give John my best. I'll call him tomorrow."

DAY SEVEN
SUNDAY MORNING

Father T slept later than usual. He had gone to bed early the night before telling his friend John Dutzow that in all his nearly 83 years he never felt so tired. As he opened his eyes and sat up in bed, he heard the kitchen door open and close just below him. It was Msgr. Dutzow going out to say the early Sunday Mass.

The priest looked out his bedroom window to the church parking lot below. It was sunny and clear. The men on the buildings and grounds committee had cleared the walks of drifting snow, and there were a few cars beginning to park in the recently plowed lot. "I wonder what the temperature is," Father T said to himself. "It must be really cold. I hope no one tries to walk to church this morning. That could be very dangerous."

Making his way downstairs, Father T could tell that his left leg was stiff and weak. He held on to the handrail for fear he might fall. "Stay with me, Lord," he prayed softly addressing the Sacred Heart of Jesus. "I still have work to do before I'm ready to slow down and move into St. Ambrose with Vinnie."

The drip coffeemaker was doing its duty, and the pastor was saying his morning prayers at the kitchen table, when the rectory phone rang.

"Good morning, St. Roch," Father T answered. He assumed that someone from out of town was calling about

Mass times.

"Father, this is Bob Taormina. I hope I'm not disturbing you. I have more news about John Urbansky's case."

"What is it, Bob? I talked to John's attorney last night and he told me that the charges have been dropped due to insufficient evidence."

"Actually, there were never any charges filed. Your friend was being held 'officially' as a material witness in a case that concerned espionage, the sharing of state secrets with a foreign government."

"Ridiculous!"

"Yes, but unfortunately there were some powerful people who used Mr. Urbansky as a diversion in the hopes that the case against him would turn the government's attention away from themselves. Frankly, I can't believe they thought they could get away with it, but that's what happened."

"Can you tell me who these people are and what they were trying to get away with?" Father T asked.

"Unfortunately, no. All I can say for sure is that they were high-ranking government officialswho were trying to court favor with a foreign government. The information they shared illegally and everything else connected with this case is classified as Top Secret. Even John and his attorney are being kept in the dark—with assurances that the investigation is over and that John's good name will be restored."

"I had a feeling (a dream actually)," Father T told him, "that this nonsense was nothing more than Washington bureaucrats trying to cover their butts by casting blame on an honest man. We have a saying, Roberto, that clearly applies to this situation, and too many others like it. Do you remember Msgr. Adrian. He was pastor at St. Roch when you were a boy. We called him The Boss. One of his favorite sayings was *'Genuit porci porcos"* (Pigs beget pigs). He distrusted bureaucrats and politicians of all stripes, and he was right. Far too often, they're only interested in maintaining the status quo and protecting their own turf no matter who gets hurt. What they did to John is a pitiful example of what government pigs will do when they're determined to put their own interests ahead of the common good."

"I can't disagree with you, Father, but in all fairness, the majority of government employees—especially my colleagues at the FBI—are people of integrity. I trust them with my life every day of the week!"

"Of course, Roberto, in my nearly 83 years of life I have worked with hundreds of government officials who were the salt of the earth, including you and many more like you. The Boss was not trying to impugn the integrity of all politicians and civil servants. But he had a particular distaste for the few rotten apples who spoil they barrel, and if you'll excuse the mixed metaphor, he could smell them at 100 paces—500 paces if he happened to be down wind. That's why he called them pigs!"

"Well the good news is that your friend John is now home with his wife and family, and the State Department has issued a press release that absolves him from all suspicion of wrongdoing. I know that doesn't make up for the injuries done to the Urbansky family by a handful of corrupt government officials, but it's a step in the right direction."

"I'm very grateful to you, Bob. This has been a tough week for me, and I'm especially glad to have John Urbansky's case officially closed!"

"You're very welcome, Father. It's the least I can do to

repay you for everything you've done for our family and for this community."

"Roberto, what can I tell John's friends here? Many people have been praying for him, and they'll be eager to hear the news."

"Father, you know I can't authorize you to disclose even the little information I've given you. Let me tell you the 'official story' being released by the State Department. It won't help you answer your friends' questions but at least it will affirm John's innocence."

The "official story" that FBI agent Taormina told the priest was not very enlightening, but it was enough to satisfy the Urbansky family members and friends. John Urbansky was officially cleared. End of story.Father T had a smile on his face as he headed over to church, and he was overheard by several parishioners as he prayed in Italian, *Mille grazie, Sacro Cuore di Gesu!*"

It felt odd to be on the altar as a concelebrant while his friend Msgr. John Dutzow said the two Sunday morning Masses; but Father T had insisted on being there. He had never missed a Sunday Mass in his nearly 60 years as a priest, and he wanted to show that the rumors about his incapacitated state were greatly exaggerated.

At the end of both Masses, Father T read the announcements. Then he added a special word of thanks to the Sacred Heart of Jesus for keeping the members of St. Roch Parish safe during the polar vortex, for the successful rescue of little Theresa Baglione at St. Ambrose, and for the release of his good friend John Urbansky who was falsely accused of espionage by the bureaucrats in Washington. He thought to himself, but did not say out loud, The Boss's frequent observation that pigs beget pigs (*Genuit porci porcos*).

After the 11 o'clock Mass, Father T and Msgr. Dutzow joined Father Mike and Msgr. Cugino at the Osteria for Sunday brunch. The sun was shining, and the temperature was rising to double digits for the first time in more than a week.

"I still don't understand why the government accused John Urbansky of spying for terrorists," Msgr. Dutzow said. "It makes no sense."

"Syria," Father T replied remembering the 'official story' told to him by Agent Taormina.

"What about Syria?" his cousin asked.

"Bob Taormina called me this morning with more-detailed information. It seems that John and Marge have good friends who came to this country 10 years ago from Syria and settled in the Urbanskys' neighborhood. Evidently members of this Syrian couple's family back home have close ties to terrorist organizations like ISIS."

"But what does that have to do with John?" Msgr. Dutzow asked.

"I can answer that," said Father Mike Belcamp. "There is real confusion in the State Department over the vetting of Syrian refugees and people seeking asylum from the brutal regime of Bashar al-Assad. Terrorist organizations have freely admitted that they are using our refugee resettlement programs to sneak radical jihadists into the U. S."

"I still don't get the connection to John Urbansky," Msgr. Dutzow said.

"According to Bob Taormina's sources in the FBI's Washington bureau," Father T said, "the Urbansky's friends don't own a computer so they frequently use John's computer at home to communicate with family and friends in Syria. That raised a red flag for the State Department techies who monitor people who have the kind of satellite access that John Urbansky has. They assumed John was sending classified information to terrorist organizations in Syria. Of course, when the techies thoroughly examined John's computer they discovered that the Syrian neighbors' communications were completely harmless. The rest is sadly comic history."

"Unbelievable!"

"What a classic case of government screw up!"

"Our tax dollars at work."

"Yes," Father T said, "but all's well that ends well. Thanks to the Sacred Heart!"

"What about John's reputation?" Msgr. Cugino asked. "Does he have to live under a permanent shadow now?"

"The FBI has announced that John Urbansky has been cleared of all suspicion. Sadly, his innocence will not be breaking news for *The Washington Post* or the nightly news, but at least it's now a matter of public record, " Father T said.

"Gentlemen, coffee cups up! Let's toast John Urbansky and his family," Msgr. Cugino said.

"C'ent anni!" They all replied, raising their cups. "May they live 100 years!"

"And speaking of 100 years," Father T exclaimed, "let's thank the Sacred Heart for allowing all of us to survive the winter storm of the century! May we never have to experience a polar vortex again!" End of Story.

49666778R00069

Made in the USA
Charleston, SC
02 December 2015